TELLER

MICHELE PACKARD

PRAISE FOR TELLER

"What's not to love about a strong female protagonist who has the ability to admire the decor of a room during a gun battle? Matti's wicked sense of humor and impeccable taste add much to this suspenseful and exhilarating novel."

— *Tresa P.*

"Matti Baker is a bad ass!! She and the other characters come to life on every page. The use of current events, government agencies, and artificial intelligence makes the book read more like non-fiction. Could this be real?"

— *Lisa M.*

"Matti Baker has blown up, and this book quite literally starts with a bang and doesn't tie up until the thirst for revenge is quenched! Taking it personally is only one step forward in the race to save America from an international conspiracy, and this secret agent woman has been doing her cardio. The grapes of wrath are pressed, fermented, and drank for breakfast, the Lion's saved by the mouse who took down the bear and the dragon, and this time, the hare beats the tortoise."

– *Tripp A.*

Thank you for your support!

PRAISE FOR PACKARD'S AESOP SERIES

"Unlike most stories involving female operatives, there is no sense of victim or subservience in Matti's world. She's at the top of her game and controls chaos itself, outsmarting the cleverest of adversaries and the political forces behind them. These elements place Matti's adventures above and beyond most thrillers featuring female protagonists."

— *Diane*

"This author is Aesop the second for she is a true storyteller. Not my usual genre. I am so glad I stepped out of my box. Now I am on top of it dancing that I read a fantastic book. What a ride. Nonstop action."

— *Trollhair*

"This is the 1st book I've read written Michele Packard; she has done a great job at writing a good book; I will definitely be reading more of her books. The story line caught my attention at the very beginning and kept me interested throughout the entire book. I loved the chemistry between the characters."

— *Jeanne*

"This book is about a contractor for the government that is a cross between Wonder Woman and Superman. She is incredible with the things she can pull off. I enjoyed the change of pace between this type of storyline and characters and the rest of the books I have read. I think anyone that likes a truly different type of book will like this book also."

— *RCF*

"This is a very compelling book with Matti Baker as the main character, amazing that she is. This book is a continuation of the previous book Aesop which was also awesome."

— *Dr. P*

ACKNOWLEDGEMENTS

This book is dedicated to my mother.

There are a bunch of writers on my father's side
and my Aunt Liz is a great storyteller,
but my mother was the Original Storyteller.
RIP Patty Jo

To every reader who purchases:
Thank you for your support and hope you enjoy the adventures.

Carpe diem!

PRELUDE

If you want peace, prepare for war.
— General Publius Flavius Vegetius Renatus

Hell hath no fury like a woman scorned.
— William Congreve

NOT ALL MISSIONS ARE THE SAME. Trust me on this. I have been working on this one for over two years. An unprecedented and terrifying plot involving the United States' own government agencies working with other countries to eradicate millions and establish a new world order.

Seriously, what type of person comes up with these elaborate conspiracies? There's mentally sick, or just downright evil. I was dealing with both.

Winston Churchill is often credited as being the original person who stated, "Those who cannot remember the past are condemned to repeat it," but in fairness, this was stated forty years prior by George Santayana.

I've immersed myself in the knowledge of history, name origins, and psychological attributes in vain attempts to learn from the past to understand the reasons why people (or countries) behave the way they do, so I can respond and remedy our nation's defense. Despite decades of training and countless missions, one thing has become clear: I have no f'in clue why people do some of the things they do, but I'm good at stopping them from doing it again.

Another thing I know…I'm not wired like everyone else. I don't think that's a bad thing, but this also lends itself to being problematic, at times, for connecting with or understanding others. Most certainly, this was a trait the United States government sought when they enlisted my help. Although I work with the help of others, I act as an independent contributor.

The more I get involved in this latest mission, the more questions I'm asking, with the shocking connections I'm encountering indicating that I am seemingly the root of it all.

Not only do I feel compelled to protect my country, but I'm duty-bound to investigate and do whatever it takes not to get caught from the very agencies that originally enlisted my services.

I've been forced to produce my own form of isolationism, so to speak, and if you follow history, you know how well that worked out for the United States.

Depeche Mode's *Policy of Truth* plays in my head…*"It's too late to change events, It's time to face the consequence, for delivering the proof, in the policy of truth…"*

I have my own quote, not as elaborate as General Publius Flavius Vegetius Renatus or William Congreve…

"Guns up!" – Matti Baker

ONE

Open Your Eyes

Open your eyes.

AS MUCH AS I TRIED, I couldn't open my eyes. They felt heavy, as if they were glued shut…or I was drugged. I kept repeating to myself *"Open your eyes,"* not in the sweet voice like Penelope Cruz in *Vanilla Sky*, but like the screaming voice of Gunnery Sergeant Hartman in *Full Metal Jacket*.

Open your eyes!

I couldn't, though.

Focus. Where are you? How did you get here? What was last thing you remember? Use your other senses, fool.

I tried to calm my mind and my nerves. My heart was pounding. *Slow it down. Breathe in, breathe out.*

Again.

Again.

Now, think.

I first tried to move my hands, but they were constrained by something. I was unable to move them. I then tried my feet, but came to the same conclusion. My body was fastened to something. I could feel something like a strap over my chest and another, also, over my knees.

Deep breath in, listen.

I could hear a repetitive beep, fast then slower. I strained to hear more. I heard a water droplet. One, two, and it kept dropping. There was a TV on, but the volume was low. I couldn't make out the words. I heard distant conversations, but the words were all jumbled. I could hear and feel a throbbing in my head.

Focus.

I smelled something familiar. I wasn't in an interrogation room; it was too sterile. Hospital. I'm in a hospital room.

Open your eyes.

I still couldn't open them.

Think! What is the last thing you remember?

I could sense I was smiling, my body and mind relaxing and recalling, despite me being restrained. I was with my husband, Tom, and Bethany, my best friend. We were at our favorite restaurant in San Francisco. We had been AWOL for almost a month, prepping for our next mission. My commander, Freddy, had just arrived, and was sporting the incognito look of Sean Connery. He motioned for us to follow him to a private room. There were two shadows in the back corner that I couldn't make out.

Oh, wait...I'm starting to remember.

My pulse was elevating. I could hear the monitors increase, uncontrollable tears now flowing from my eyes, but I still couldn't open them. My stomach was caving in, and there was a heavy pressure on my chest and a lump in my throat. I was choking on my own tears.

Stop, please, I can't.

It was my parents. I hadn't seen them in such a long time. I remember being so euphoric upon seeing their faces. I knew they had made sacrifices to be here. I remember being shocked to see them, but was smiling, as I was so happy by the surprise. The full circle of life was coming to conclusion. They were my adopted parents, but to me, they were my only parents. My birth mother died, and she instructed Freddy to deliver me to them. She was my birth mother's sister. After decades, I recently found out that Freddy was my biological father. He felt so much anguish from the physical and emotional torture I endeared over the years that he wanted to surprise me before we left for another long mission, and this was his peace offering.

I can still feel their hugs and kisses as we reminisced. It was surreal. We just sat down and ordered a bottle of Hundred Acre cabernet, filling each other in on life. I remember we were all laughing.

I can't. Stop! Please stop. I'm starting to remember.

I had a photo of our three children that I had been meaning to mail to my parents. We recently took the photo when we dropped them off to training camp. I wanted to give it to my parents. I knew they would be proud to see how they had grown and learn what they were doing. I excused myself to go to our car to get it. I had parked the car a block away as a security precaution, and remember thinking that the four-inch heels I was wearing were killing me. I was going through our bags to see if I could find a more comfortable pair. I had been gone roughly ten minutes.

No, no, please don't make me remember.

I had just closed the car door, clicked "lock" on the remote, and was walking back when I first saw the reflection in another car window. I remember seeing the red and yellow glow of detonation in the window before I even heard the blast or felt the pressure catapult me over the car hood. I must have been blown ten feet from my original spot. My head slammed into the street sign; my arms crossed over my body in a futile attempt to eliminate further injuries. My body was in slow motion while my mind was racing. I had to get up. How much time had passed? It seemed like forever. I pushed myself up and landed back down, hard, onto the pavement, then tried it again. I had to go back. I pulled on the bent street pole to lift myself up slowly, ever so slowly. The smoke and fumes from the explosion were blinding, overpowering. I was coughing, and my eyes burned. There was debris everywhere. Cars were turned over, glass was all around me, and buildings held large new openings.

Don't look.

The new heels I just put on were no longer on. My left side was scraped, and a three-inch piece of glass stuck out of my thigh. My index finger was sliced through to the bone. Blood was sluggishly oozing—I just wasn't sure from how many places.

I had no idea how much time had passed. I was slowly attempting to make my way back when a first responder stopped me in the middle of the road.

"Ma'am, you've been in an accident. We need to take you in for medical attention."

I tried to comprehend what he was saying. I focused on his mouth, but couldn't make out the words.

"I have to get to my family. They are in the restaurant." I thought I said that whole sentence, but the only thing he could understand was, "Family…restaurant."

"Ma'am, you can't go to the restaurant right now. You have serious injuries; we need to take you to an ambulance."

"I have to get my family at the restaurant," I stammered.

I remember.

His eyes were remorseful. He placed his arm behind my back to hold me steady, looked me in the eyes, and said, "Ma'am, that's where the blast originated. No one there survived." My knees gave way, and he carried me to the ambulance.

If only it stopped there. I know why I can't open my eyes.

I was lying on a gurney in the middle of the hall. Medical personnel were racing, frantic, assessing who to treat first. New people on stretchers were coming in. Most wouldn't make it. Police and fire were there, too, bringing more and more casualties. Lifeless bodies, lifeless eyes, missing body parts. Not enough time to even respectfully cover these beings, as attendees were trying to confirm identities. I looked at each knowing that eventually I would see my family. I didn't want to see.

My eyes fixed on the TV, trying to see what had happened. Close captioning was on, as the commotion from the rooms was deafening. I read as the reports came in, confirming there were no survivors at the immediate location. They estimated over seventy-five casualties from the direct and indirect impact of the blast.

I didn't want to process it. My eyes continued to flow uncontrollably. I was still watching the TV as I saw the nurse walk over to me to assess my injuries. "We're going to take good care of you. Can you tell me who you are?" she asked. I was transfixed on the TV. I couldn't respond. I was in a comatose state. There were reports of another explosion which they were trying to confirm. No survivors. The nurse asked me again what my name was. I continued staring at the tv monitor. Finally, they listed the location…a remote training facility outside Minot Airforce Base.

A gut-wrenching howl, deep from the depravity of my soul, exploded. I screamed hysterically for my children. Thrashing about on the gurney, I yelled incomprehensibly before she stuck the needle into the side of my neck. Then there was nothing.

I remember. Please God, no.

Everyone was dead. My parents, my husband, my best friend,

my commander—all in one fell swoop. And, now my children, who were at training. They took them ALL from me. I was the unknowing designated survivor. Nat King Cole's *Unforgettable* played over and over in my head…"*Unforgettable, that's what you are. Unforgettable, though near or far…*"

PLEASE, God, wake me up from this hell!

There are moments that change us, pain that you can't escape. I had no idea how long I was out. My eyes still shut. It was too soon to open them. I didn't want to open them. I couldn't face my new reality.

My mind drifted amongst memories. How Bethany and I met in training when we were just sixteen; how I met Tom at Chateau Marmont and knew he was the love of my life; the kid's premature arrival on 9/11; figuring out that Freddy was my real Dad…the memories kept coming. I was confused, thinking… *"We're in the spirit world, Chavez,"* mixing fiction with reality.

A person will black out things he doesn't want to remember, pain that must be escaped from – even if temporary.

I remember. I remember it all.

The nurses and doctors had strapped me in for my protection. They couldn't decipher a word I said. I had no identification on me, and the best they could ascertain, my family was now dead. The tears continued to flow.

Open your eyes.

I continued going back and forth from reality in my trance state. I tried to think of something that would help me relax and thought about the movie *Shawshank Redemption*… "*Hope is a good thing. Maybe the best of things. Get busy living or get busy dying.*"

Hope is about self-preservation. Our survival instinct is our single greatest source of inspiration. I had no hope. I wanted my family. If there's one thing I had learned, it's that an enemy who doesn't care about the future is hard to battle. Inside my tormented self, the rage was building. As God as my witness, they would all pay.

My eyes started to twitch, fluttering to open. The hot tears still streamed. The time had come. I heard the song by Imagine Dragons pounding in my head…"*I'm waking up. Welcome to the new age…*"

TWO

Eyes Wide Open

I SAT THERE, SCANNING THE ROOM. I had on a blue and white gown and wore yellow socks. I had an IV drip going, a heart monitor beeping, and a TV/bed remote close to my secured left hand. Directly in front of me was a mirror with a small sink. I could see a bandage covering my head. There were bloodstains on it, so either no one had taken the liberty to change it, or it was fresh blood.

There were no flowers or cards. Everyone I cared about was dead. No one would be coming for me. The benefit I had was, they thought I was dead, too. They'd wish I was dead by the time I was done.

There was a walk-in bathroom, exit door, a wall, and a large see-through window for monitoring. The nurse's station was catty-corner from my view, so I could see what they were doing.

I had no idea how much time had passed. Hours? Days? I had no recollection of time, but needed to know the answer. I pressed the call button on the remote and a nurse arrived shortly thereafter.

"I'm so glad to see you awake. How are you feeling? Can I get you anything?" she asked sincerely and gingerly.

"What day is it? How long have I been out?" I stammered.

"It's 8 am. You've been out for almost 8 hours. You didn't have any identification on you, and there were no fingerprints on file.

What is your name, honey? We have a few people who need to talk to you."

I paused. "Scotti."

"Hi, Scotti. I'm Alicia, and I'll be your nurse 'til 7 pm tonight. I promise to take good care of you."

"Alicia, can we please take off these restraints?" I struggled to say.

"I wish I was authorized to do so, but I'll need to get clearance from the doctor. He's on rounds right now, but should be back shortly."

"Can I get you anything now? Are you in any pain?"

"A water and some pain meds. My head is throbbing."

"Ok, sweetie, let me go get that and bring it back, and then I'll contact downstairs to come get your information."

I had roughly ten minutes to get out of these restraints and make it past the nurses' station. I couldn't afford to be here any longer. Any Jane Doe notifications would be sending out signals to the wrong parties. A Jane Doe with multiple scars over her entire body would escalate that quickly. I was surprised the police weren't here already. They must still be consumed with the other casualties.

I lost count of how many surgeries and bumps and bruises I'd acquired over the years. Some were to be expected, others—I happened to be at the wrong place at the wrong time. The last time, I was physically rebuilt. It took me six months in the hospital and another six months in seclusion to recover. That event was the genesis of the loss of my entire family.

Dual double agents had been tracking me to obtain lethal vials that I possessed after my mother's death. We concluded they wanted them for a select genocide. The conspiracy grew as we tied in direct involvement of the CIA, NSA, Russia, China, and the

Middle East. Hell, even TSA was suspected of being involved. The question became, who *wasn't* involved? Someone(s) wanted me dead for what I'd possessed and concealed decades ago.

Being a private counterterrorism operative, I have the luxury of taking on assignments that I choose. I didn't choose this. I've been trained to assist government and outside agencies in identifying, locating, and, if necessary, eliminating individuals or nations that pose threats to the US. Who knew it was an inside job…?

The Deputy Director of the CIA, a member of House of Representatives, and the dual double agents were just eliminated. It was necessary. I envisioned Tom Bale, Scott Bartik, Fareed and Abdul Webb holding hands in hell.

I made the mistake of not eliminating Paul Rogers, the Director of the NSA. In return, he killed or assisted in killing everyone who was important to me.

I would become like Arya Stark in *Game of Thrones*: a faceless enemy making a kill list and checking it twice, reminding all parties involved, "*What do we say to the God of Death? …not today.*"

I needed to stop reminiscing and focus. I had five minutes before the nurse returned. My left hand was double jointed, and I popped it out of the cuff quickly. From there, I loosened the chest and leg straps and got my hand out of the right cuff. My clothes were not visible, so they were either in the bathroom or I was going to have to switch with the nurse, who I calculated to be three sizes larger than me. That was the least of my problems.

I placed my hands under the cuffs, causing my finger to throb. Upon her arrival, she'd lifted my bed to a sitting position and gave me a sip of water through a straw. She then entered in my medication on the computer and injected a painkiller into my IV. She promptly asked if I needed anything else before the doctor returned. I looked at the vacated nurse's station and asked for another sip of water. I purposely dribbled on my gown, and she grabbed a tissue and bent close to wipe it up.

You see it in the movies, but it really requires a trained person to perform a central nervous system shutdown. When struck in the neck adjacent to a person's Adam's Apple, a person passes out from 'false' extreme high blood pressure. The brain is tricked to thinking it's high blood pressure, when it's not, and will autocorrect in attempts to lower it, which results in the person fainting. Easy peasy—well, if you are trained.

Alicia went down like a brick on top of my legs. I promptly sat up, readjusted her into the bed, got up, yanked the IV out, and searched the bathroom. My black Gucci pantsuit was hanging on a hook, albeit ruined, with a large rips and covered in gray ash. I slipped it on and took Alicia's scrub shirt off to wear over it. I yanked the head bandage off, so had quite the look going. Luckily, Alicia had a $20 bill in her pocket (probably lunch money), so I kept that too. I secured her in the same straps I had been in and yanked the bed chords from the power outlets. I took her socks and made a gag so she wouldn't be screaming before I got away. Sorry, Alicia.

I put on her size eleven croc-like shoes. *Damn, these are pretty comfy, actually. WTF! I must be in shock.* I looked out the wall window, saw that I had a small opening of time to get to the exit, and away I went.

Once on the main floor, I ducked and maneuvered to the front exit. I took a ball cap and backpack from the waiting room area and scored sunglasses in the process. I only had moments before Alicia would awaken. There was no telling if someone had already found her. *Please, God, give me a break.*

The white Nissan Sentra with the Uber/Lift sign in the front windshield came strolling up to let out a passenger. I briskly walked towards it and stated I'd just lost my phone, but only needed a ride 5 minutes away to the Fairmont Hotel. Step one, done.

Upon entering the hotel, I went to the lobby phone and ordered additional towels for my room. Once the maid arrived and started entering, I followed after her and thanked her for dropping off the towels, and even had $3 left to tip her.

I quickly showered and dressed and tried to evaluate my options. *They are all dead.* The tears continued to flow, adding to a crippling pain in my chest and stomach as I bent over and sobbed.

My subconscious knew I didn't have time to cry. Lacking information, it could only be a matter of time before my enemies would know that I'd survived. I wasn't even positive who they were, but knew they had the means. I knew I had to get out of California and bring the fight to where I could control it. I needed time, and I needed resources.

I grabbed a few necessary items from the room—various passports, a burner phone, a shitload of cash, a blonde wig—and wondered where Tom's passports were. *He must have left them in the car.* I didn't have time to retrieve them, and it didn't matter now. Flock of Seagulls was going through my mind "…*and I ran, I ran so far away…*".

I left everything else behind, including my dead family. I was no longer Matti Baker. She'd died with them.

THREE

Solo

ARRIVING AT SAN FRANCISCO AIRPORT, I scanned departing flights from each airline. I'd be flying commercial and needed as little red flags as possible. The first problem was that I was paying in cash right now, until I could secure my other belongings. NSA and Financial Crimes Enforcement Network (FinCen) were created to help law enforcement identify money laundering and other illegal activity, and to stop terrorism by tracking purchases. I was counting on this later, versus now.

It looked like my best option was to fly American. I booked a flight to DFW under my new name, Scotti Worthington. I choose this name because one of my first assignments was with this kooky wine couple who purchased a bottle of Screaming Eagle for $500,000. Bless their hearts. They were Jon and Sara Worthington, but I didn't look like a Sara, so opted for the name of Scotti.

First class wasn't available. FML. I had a small purse-like bag that the ticket counter agent wanted to charge me to put in the overhead bin. *Are you fucking crazy?* Had airlines really stooped to this level? Had I not been through enough already? Good grief.

Bethany had coordinated most of my travel plans before or piloted the aircrafts herself. We'd been best friends since age sixteen. She took care of my husband and my kids when I had my FUBAR episode that premeditated all this. *Oh Bethany, I'm so sorry. Please forgive me.*

I was in the last row, middle seat. May have well just put me in the toilets. It was a four-hour flight, which I used to source through any news intel I could. The media was reporting that the detonation in San Francisco was due to a gas leak coupled with an eighteen-wheeler shipment of petroleum headed for the harbor. The detonation by Minot AFB was because a chopper crashed-landed on explosive military supplies. No one would link them together because there was no reason to suspect foul play. I couldn't log into my server, so had to rely on public sources. The misinformation the media feeds the public is alarming on all levels. I cringe when people cite Twitter as their source, when only two percent of the US population uses it.

Two hours into the flight, I visibly jolted out of my seat when I thought about Jake and Steve. Holy shit, how could I have not even thought about them until now? *Maybe because you lost your parents, real dad, husband, best friend, and children?!* I was momentarily relieved. I was not all alone after all. Tears streamed down my face uncontrollably while my body shook.

Jake and Steve were an extension of me. We had met when they were in Seals training and we instantly became best friends. They have helped me on various missions and were intricately involved in this last mission. For now, I couldn't contact them. I wouldn't risk their lives, and I know they voluntarily would. I needed more time, more intel.

Oh God, I forgot about the dogs, too! More tears continued to flow, and the passengers beside me were becoming nervous about my reactions. I apologized to them and informed them, in my best Texas accent, that I'd just found out my momma had died.

Our family had four dogs. Two trained attack German shepherds that I acquired after FUBAR, and two somewhat overweight labs that the family acquired in my absence. I loved those dogs. They were being reluctantly boarded until Tom and I finalized a new residence in San Francisco. My heart expanded, knowing they were alive.

Upon landing in DFW, I purchased a first-class ticket to Naples that was departing in one hour. The twelve-hour flight cost me $12,000. What a rip-off. I could practically fly chartered for that. I carefully watched the TSA agents to ensure no one was observing me. I crawled into my seat and, due to the physical and emotional pain, passed out for the duration of the flight.

FOUR

Altra Famiglia

UPON ARRIVAL IN NAPLES, I was punctually greeted by Aldo. He shook my hand, picked up my small bag, and escorted me to a new Mercedes Maybach. I met Aldo over twenty years ago and formed a lasting friendship and alliance with this personable gentleman. His demeanor was more of a kind-hearted grandfather. Lean, 6'0, grey hair and mustache, dressed in a black business suit, now roughly seventy years old, you wouldn't have suspected that Aldo was one of the "High Camorra." Yes, my friends, the Italian mafia is very much alive and thriving.

The Camorra mafia is most active in Naples, but controls down to Southern Italy with their allies, the Sicilian mafia. Their outreach extends to neighboring countries—Spain, Germany, Albania, Africa, and yes, the United States of America. A few of their known activities involve drug trafficking, prostitution, waste management, smuggling, bid rigging, and murder. It was for this last category that I would be enlisting their services.

"Matti, it's a pleasure to see you again. I was pleasantly surprised when you reached out."

"Aldo, it's always a pleasure to see you. I wish I was here under different circumstances."

"Pray tell, my friend. You were vague in your requests."

"I'll need to retrieve my belongings I left here with you, and thank you for taking me to Ravello to solicit some additional support."

"All of your belongings?"

"Yes, I'm afraid so. Of course, I'll pay the customary fee in advance."

"No need for that, we can settle when it's all done."

I loved that about this country. They didn't worry about the incidental things. If you went into a store and didn't have the right change for something, they just tell you to make it up to them later. When you check into a hotel, you don't need to worry about putting down a credit card. They know where to find you.

"Your message was brief. Care to elaborate a bit during the ride?" he sincerely inquired.

"Suffice it to say, they made it personal. They killed my entire family in one fell swoop."

"I see. I understand, dear child. No need to say more, we'll be here to assist in whatever manner you deem necessary. I already alerted the others to assemble, per your request."

"Grazie mille, Aldo."

The drive from Naples to Ravello is breathtaking from the small winding roads along the coastline. Although I consider myself an expert driver, these people here are the real professionals, with streets so tiny they calculate the distance between cars by the millimeters. For many foreigners, or those unaccustomed to it, the speed and precision with which they take the roads can be unnerving; especially the one-lane roads for dual passage. Typically, drivers tend to take visitors via the route through Pompei and down south to Positano, for the views. Today, Aldo took me through the extremely curvy roads of Corbara, which suggest the original architect was on some serious LSD when they engineered these passages. Aldo maneuvered expertly, as if he was a Grand Prix driver.

Aldo dropped me off at Hotel Rufolo, located on the outer perimeter of the center of the piazza. It was a quaint hotel, with cascading pink bougainvillea draping down the entrance, positioned high so you could view the Tyrrhenian Sea.

"I'll see you at 10," he informed me when he opened the door to escort me in.

"Until then, my friend."

As I had no belongings, I left to scout for some new clothes and necessities, which I quickly acquired in the local shops only footsteps away from the hotel entrance. Italian linen was not generally my first choice of wardrobe, but with my flowing blonde locks, it did offer quite an appeal. Heels are not generally worn, due to the cobblestone streets, so I opted for some elegant sandals by Salvatore Ferragamo which, honestly, was a better option for me right now, due to the wound that I was nursing on my thigh. I also procured some Rocky S2V special ops boots and other necessary gear in an underground store.

At 9:55 pm, I left to walk to the restaurant Campa Cosimo. Its outside appearance was of a traditional Italian trattoria. Inside, white tablecloth-adorned tables were in close proximity of each other for an intimate surrounding. It's a family-owned business, with Momma still proudly checking the tables and making sure you have enough to eat while the sons, the technical owners, welcome and cater to the guests' every whim. Italians eat late. You can always tell who the foreigners are, as they arrive between 6:30-7:30 pm.

It was a relatively light night attendance-wise, and I was escorted to the back room where Aldo was already present. He introduced me to Bessum, the head of the Albanian mafia, and Lily, who was representing the Sicilian family due to her husband's recent incarceration. Bessum ("Bes") was probably in his mid-fifties, just under six feet, and stocky, with piercing green eyes that were instinctively and intuitively watching every move. Like a hawk. Lily was a refined elegant beauty, more like royalty. Early forties, long black hair, stunning huge brown eyes, dressed to the hilt, and draped in diamonds.

I requested we keep the party to a minimum, for discretion. Bes and Lily embraced me with a hug and kissed each cheek, as if we were long lost friends. I detected that Bes was carrying a Springfield 9mm during his embrace, and was confident that Lily was carrying, too. She looked like a Glock person, to me.

We sat and were promptly served with a smorgasbord of delectable appetizers, plus the traditional bread and olive oil, with oversized wine glasses filled with their personal selection of Sassicaia. There were no menus provided. They would be presenting their selections to us, while leaving us to attend to business.

Aldo turned to me and said, "Now that pleasantries are done...Matti..."

"First, thank each of you for coming to hear me out. Aldo, my sincere appreciation to you for organizing things so quickly, and for your discretion and friendship over the years. Bes, Lily...thank you for allowing me to present a situation that could prove beneficial for each party present."

Bes was quick to point out, "I can't speak for Lily, but for me and our organization, I'm present to "hear," and in no way guarantee participation or cooperation at this point."

"Certainly. I wouldn't expect otherwise. All I ask is an opportunity to present and explain."

"Let her finish, Bes, before you jump the gun, as always," Lily protested as she feigned annoyance.

Aldo quietly laughed and commented, "Matti, I should clarify that I contacted Bes and Lily not only due to their discretion and competence, but also due to their unique relationship. They are cousins."

"Ah, well, I thank you both, and I understand the importance of family – the reason you are here is because someone took my family from me. All of them. My three parents, my husband, my best friend..." I started to choke up, so paused momentarily before adding "... and my three children."

There's one thing you don't mess with for Italians or Albanians...and that's family. Farah Fawcett in *Burning Bed* had nothing on them. More like Lorena Bobbitt, cutting off his manhood, shoving it in his mouth, and burning him slowly in his bed while they made him watch as they raped and tortured the other family members in front of him. Including the dog. Just saying.

"Poor dear, who would do such a thing?" Lily inquired.

"That's my dilemma. I'm not sure, but it's more than one party, and its origin is both inside and outside of the US."

For the next hour and a half, I proceeded to disclose the particulars of the last eighteen months. The speculation and conspiracy involvement of CIA, NSA, China, Russia, the Middle East, the seven scientists, the twin theory, and even the Illuminati.

Each sat there momentarily, trying to process. Aldo was the first to respond. "Matti, that's quite a list. I feel it's prudent to share with the others why you are being targeted, besides your investigation, interrogation, and participation with the parties involved."

There was only six people who knew that I possessed lethal vials that my mother had stolen and left to me upon her demise.

These vials were a matter of national security, and would cause global genocide if they were distributed in a world-wide solution via air, water, or (my theory) wine consumption.

"Aldo, in my lifetime, there have only been six people I have discussed this with. Of the six, you are the only one still alive."

"Yes, I understand the significance, but Bes and Lily need to know, too. They deserve to receive the whole picture so they can to determine their participation level and commitment."

I spent another ten minutes filling them on how I came into possession of the vials. Lily was first to ask, "Where are they now?"

"No one except me knows of their location. I'm not willing to share any more at this time. In the event of my untimely death, should they be found and procured, it would be at the destruction of these individuals and the country. I can assure you that it will not be your country, or any of your present allies."

"Present? Interesting adjective," Bes commented.

"Friendships change over the years and centuries. I can't guarantee forever, but I can guarantee I will hold responsible those that took my family from me."

"There's much on the table to consider, as well as the ramifications to us as individuals, and our organization. I need more to even consider this. It's not helping to hear the forecasted economic woes of your nation, the ramblings of your President, or the daily mass shootings in your own nation."

"Well, that's a perfect segue that allows me to deliberate a different scenario. It's been over eighteen years since the 9/11 attacks. The loss of life was substantial, but the real casualty was the long-term economic impact and the divisiveness between parties and classes who are rooted by fear. School shootings are now, sadly, a daily occurrence. Democrats and Republicans are unable to come to any agreement for solutions. Personally, I consider lobbyists to be a fundamental problem that creates these scenarios, but that's another issue all together. What better way to strike fear than to have your own people killing each other? We can argue the merits of gun control and putting in much-needed restrictions, but it would take decades for that to have any meaningful impact. School shooters have been primarily white males in both political parties. As social media has grown in popularity, shootings have skyrocketed. It doesn't matter that the numbers are significantly insignificant compared to the daily casualties caused by medical errors, suicide, car accidents, the flu, or homicides. What both parties do agree on is that these individuals, these shooters, had specific defined mental situations that were not identified or addressed."

"I'm not following. What are you alluding to, Matti?" probed Aldo.

"To sum up, social media rewards and allows everyone to play the blame game and directs the public's attention to the stories they want you to read. Who has recently been accused of tampering and misdirection? Russia. Now, couple that with who is the US and the world's largest pharmaceutical supplier who is entering world domination of technology? China. What more sinister way to collapse a country than to have it break itself?"

"It's just a theory at this point, with no conclusive hypothesis to support it, though. You, yourself, have stated that your own agencies are involved. Why would we get involved?" Bes asked, perplexed.

"Because your countries depend and rely on our success. Our demise...our failure on any level...will also be yours."

There was a moment of silence while each person processed the implications.

"What do you want to do, and how do you want us to assist you? There's much at stake here," asked Lily.

"You're right. There's everything at stake. How do you break an inner circle? You must break the chain. If I'm wrong, no one will be the wiser, and we'll have eliminated, at the very least, some corrupt parties. If I am right, your children can live to have their own children, and you can thank me later."

Bes proceeded, "How do you suggest we accomplish this?"

"Divide and conquer. Here's what I'm proposing...."

Playing in the background, I heard the music change from an Italian serenade to American top hits...Guns and Roses, *Welcome to the Jungle..."Welcome to the jungle, we take it day by day. If you want it, you're gonna bleed, but it's the price to pay..."*

How appropriate. I took it as sign. I just love Italy.

FIVE

Intervention

RESEARCH TELLS US that the last thing you see before death is your kids. I always wonder how they confirmed this theory. After all, you must not have died for them to inquire, which therefore means it's not the last thing you see, as you're not dead. Conundrum.

I was back in the hotel, asleep, having the most wonderful dream. My family was in Montana, outside our home, sitting around the back-patio fire pit. It was a cool evening, with star-filled skies. We were laughing about something. The dogs were chasing bunny rabbits in the back yard. Tom had decanted a delicious Asuka Cab Franc that we sipped on while we nibbled on a charcuterie board of meats and crackers. Mathew and Mark were roughhousing, while Mary was telling us stories of school and friends and laughing about recent events.

I must be dreaming.

I was so happy, watching the kids, feeling the night air, gazing at Tom. I was soaking it all in and was transfixed on the fire pit, which was bustling with red and yellow flames. *Where had I seen that before?* I watched in amazement as the flames went higher and higher. Suddenly, I could feel the mood change from contentment to terror as the flames continued to grow, unstoppable, consuming everything and everyone around them but me. I was reliving the explosion. I awoke screaming, drenched in my own sweat, surveying and fearful of my surroundings.

Dreams are an involuntary collection of memories or feelings that occur during REM sleep. Why do some people dream, while others have nightmares? Researchers think that reveries provide clues and even premonitions. When I awoke, I felt that someone was watching me. I grabbed my 1911 from under my pillow and listened. 3.2.1.

Ring, ring.

I kept my eyes glued on the window and then the door, and slowly shifted my legs off the bed.

Ring, ring.

I walked slowly and cautiously over to the desk to pick up the room phone and pressed one to answer, while maneuvering to position my back to the wall with access to the front door. "Ciao."

"Thin Lizzy," the male voice said on the other end of the line. My mind froze, conflicted and tormented.

The line was still while I hesitated. "The boys are back in town," I quietly responded.

"That's right, we are. We were going to come up, but were too scared you'd rigged the place to blow. Mind if we come join you?" Jake inquired.

I had my hand over my mouth, covering the quivering of my lips while tears flowed down my cheeks. "Give me five and I'll meet you at the pool floor. You would have been correct. I need to disarm the explosives I set on the door and windows. See you in a sec." I overheard Steve saying to Jake, as I was hanging up, "You owe me $100 and your life. I knew she would have it wired to blow."

Jake and Steve, two of the best Navy Seals, had become my lifelong family and colleagues. Both tall physical specimens, with Jake blonde-headed and Steve brown. They could pass for brothers, themselves.

Less than five minutes later, I walked towards them at the entrance of the pool. I raced the last ten feet and flung my arms over each of them as I held them in a tight embrace. I didn't want to let go.

Jake pulled back from the embrace to look at me. He brushed my hair gingerly from my face, thankfully not pressing hard on the side of my head that I'd hit. He grabbed my elbow and led me to a nearby table. Steve happily joined along, grinning from ear to ear.

"How did you find me?"

"It was a wild-ass guess at first, but we knew you had some ties here, when we came, for that op that had gone wrong," Jake started to explain.

That "op" was when I was hogtied on a yacht in Positano by the original terrorist who returned years later to assassinate me and started all this mess. Mother F'er. My only consolation was that my dogs went to town on that mangled piece of shit, and we fed him to the fishes. Literally.

I was confused about how I felt as I sat across from the boys. On one hand, I was elated, but on the other, conflicted. When your whole family is torched, trust is not necessarily a strong suit afterwards. Not to mention, I wasn't too much of a trusting person before.

"How did you track me to here?"

"Once we arrived, we started asking the locals in the square if anyone saw a striking blonde. It didn't take long before we found someone who saw you returning to this hotel," Jake replied.

"Wait. How did you know I was blonde?" I asked incredulously, with a growing scowl on my face.

"Tom told us."

My head shifted and shook slowly from side to side, trying to compute what they were saying. My nose and eyes squinched together in confusion. I pushed myself back from the table, a maneuver to allow a clearer shot, if needed. My right hand rested on the small of my back, ready to retrieve my 1911, while my left hand reached for the Ka Bar in my side pocket.

"I'm not understanding, boys. How could Tom tell you?"

Steve looked over to Jake with a frozen look and then returned his gaze to me. He pounded his fist on the table (I wasn't sure if he was happy or mad) while turning to Jake and saying, "I told you she was in the blind. She doesn't KNOW."

"Know what? And get to the point, loves. I've had a pretty traumatic week and am not the best judge in character, right now."

"Matti, please…you'll want to remain calm and look at me, with what I'm about to say. Take a deep breath." Jake waited until he could see me breathe. "They are alive. ALL of them are ALIVE."

My head was now shaking from side to side more strenuously, in confusion. "What do you mean? How could that be?"

"Freddy, your parents, Tom, Bethany…they got out of the restaurant just before the detonation. Freddy got ahold of the kids in time and got them out before the explosion. Matti, listen…ALL of them are alive."

I sat there. I didn't know how to respond. What had I just thought in the hospital? There are moments that change us…pain that you can't escape. I got up and stumbled before blacking out to the ground.

SIX

Part Deux

I FELT LIKE I HAD BEEN HIT by an eighteen-wheeler. The emotional, psychological, and physical trauma from the last few days had been excruciating and paralyzing.

I was lying on the pool chaise lounge when I awoke moments later. Jake and Steve were kneeling beside me on each side, each with solemn smiles.

"Shit, I'm never going to live this down, am I?"

"Can't say I see that happening anytime soon," Steve responded with a shit-eating grin.

"We're accustomed to carrying your sorry ass on assignments. Just didn't realize we'd be doing it so soon," Jake added with his own smirk.

Damn, just like in *Money Heist,* I'd made irrational decisions and assumptions on pieces of information based solely on what I could observe. I saw the reflection of the detonation; I saw the scroll on the TV. Decades of training went right out the window. Why? Because it was personal. I responded paranoid and irrationally, due to it. I was sickened to the core just thinking about how quickly I'd caved. F'in pathetic. My consolation was they were not dead. Otherwise, I was disgusted with myself.

Jake, the more sensitive of the two, knew what I was battling internally. "Don't beat yourself up. If the roles would have been reversed, I would have blown everyone to kingdom come by now."

"Well, that's not too far off from my intentions. Walk me through what happened, and don't spare any details."

"We can, but we have someone else arriving just now, who can do a better job explaining it than us," Steve said as he pointed to the lobby stairs.

I turned my head to watch and saw a figure emerge, one step at a time. I lifted my body from the lounger and sat up as she continued to walk my way. I knew everything about her, and she knew me as well. She could pass for a model on any given day, with strangers constantly asking if she was Robin Givens or Halle Berry. My heart was filling with joy. I had never been so happy to see her.

I got up and walked over to meet her while our eyes stayed glued on each other, large smiles now forming. We wrapped our arms around each other and just held on.

Steve looked over to Jake and commented, "I don't know about you, but I felt something move on that."

Still clinging to each other, Bethany and I bent over laughing. "Way to ruin it, as always, loser."

"I don't know about you, but I could use a drink. Let's move this party indoors," I stated as I pointed to the restaurant.

"It's 9 AM," professed Bethany.

"It's five somewhere," Jake, Steve, and I said in unison, and walked back towards the restaurant.

The hotel staff sat us in a secluded area of the restaurant and we quickly ordered and asked them to procure two bottles of a Fossati Barolo 2006. The wait staff feigned an indifference to our ordering, another reason I simply love Italy.

I realized I was still holding firmly onto Bethany's hand and reluctantly let go as we sat down.

"B, I need to talk to Tom and the kids, but I need to hear what happened first…" I trailed off.

"Well, suffice it to say, once again I have taken care of your family in time of dire need…" she started sarcastically, with a knowing and pompous smile.

"You're killing me woman. Between these two and you, it's clear to me that I need new friends."

"Ok, ok. Well…when you left the restaurant to get those pictures for your parents…Freddy received a text from an unidentified number that said, "Bet she wishes now she didn't miss that shot. Time for us to say goodbye." We got out of the restaurant in less than a minute of it exploding and were across the street, inside the bike shop. Your mom and dad had a few cuts and bruises from blown glass, but overall, they fared well for their age. Tom had a huge gash to his arm and we had to stop the bleeding, and Freddy broke his foot when he was thrown by the explosion, as he was heading up the rear of the group. I luckily managed to escape any substantial injuries, so was busy doctoring up everyone else."

She paused on that, and I impatiently prompted, "And…"

"Freddy had the foresight to immediately contact Ainsworth and arranged for the safe and immediate passage of the kids and any personnel away from the training facility. Tom left as soon as his arm was wrapped up (with his own shirt, mind you) to go look for you. With all the debris and smoke, by the time he reached the car, you weren't there. Your shoes were located under another car. We didn't know if a medic had you, or you had been taken. We did know that whoever organized it must have assumed that we had all been killed in the explosion, and we needed to use that to our advantage."

"Where is everyone now?'

"Well, Tom dropped your parents off with Tia. They are now on an extended vacation in South America. Tom and the kids are temporarily in NYC. I figured: what better way to hide, for time being, then amongst millions of strangers? Freddy is in Maryland. They are all pretty anxious to hear from you."

God bless Tia. Tia had been hired to assist in my upbringing and eventual training, when I was young. She was "family" in that Freddy had arranged for her to help protect me and my parents. I knew my parents would be in good hands, despite Tia's advancing age in her 70s. Maybe she and Aldo would be a good fit, down the road?

"Where is Rogers?" I inquired next.

"He's at NSA headquarters in Maryland. That's why Freddy is there to monitor. Status quo on his activities, for the time being."

I was noticing a trend: anything that ended with "A" was becoming problematic or was somehow entangled in this mess—CIA, NSA, TSA, DIA, Russia, China...and I... who was I kidding? FDA/DEA needed to be added to the list, now, too.

The US "Intelligence Community" has 17 agencies that fall underneath it. The six program managers include the Central Intelligence Agency (CIA), Defense Intelligence Agency (DIA), Federal Bureau of Investigations (FBI), National Geospatial Intelligence Agency (NGIA), National Reconnaissance Office (NRO), and National Security Agency (NSA).

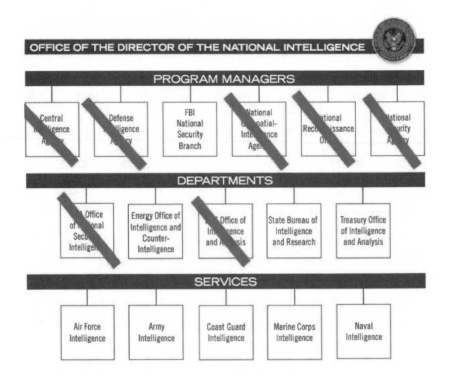

These agencies fall under the Director of National Intelligence (DNI). We had been focusing on a much smaller picture within the CIA with the demise of former Directors Carter and Bale, who had alliances with dual agents Fareed and Abdul. All are no longer breathing on this fine earth. Rogers, who was NSA, now reports to DNI.

We needed to broaden our scope. The current Director of National Intelligence is Karen Williams. She is tall woman at 5'11 with black, slicked-back hair, wired-rim glasses, and a chin that was problematic not to stare at. She wasn't attractive, unlike the actress Taraji Henson in the show *Empire* who is, but was apparently just as ruthless. I met her once. She gave me the heebie-jeebies. A damn woman, again. Don't kid yourself by thinking woman are the weaker sex. Women can be much more devious than men, from my experience.

Ever since NSA had highly classified information copied and leaked, personnel had been coming and going so fast, it was hard to keep track. The disillusioned whistleblower took asylum in, of all places, Russia. Again: an agency or country ending in an "A" that was causing internal strife that held consequences for all.

"Now that you're not dead, what are you thinking?" Bethany questioned.

"First, I need to ensure that my family is protected. After that, I solicited some local support in my brief time here. I think we need to plan timed attacks to take off the heads of this Cerberus."

I noticed that Jake and Steve both looked over to Bethany for confirmation or validation.

"What gives?" I requested.

"We have a solution for the family that we wanted to run by you. Before you balk, just listen." Bethany proceeded. I sat there motionless while she continued. "The kids want to continue training, and…"

I cut her off before she could finish. "No, not until we resolve this."

"Woman, will you let me finish?" she continued on. "We think the best persons to take care of the kids and Tom would be Jake and Steve. We have Ainsworth on board, who will help in interim, but he's getting up there in age and is ready for full-time civilian retirement. There's no one better to train them and protect them going forward, and you know that."

I looked towards Jake and Steve. "How could you manage that and your professional workload?"

Steve responded first. "We've been talking retirement for a

while now, and thinking about going into the private sector. Looks like there's an opening that pays well. We have ideas to modify the program and expand it long term. It will be just as grueling…and rewarding."

"Oh, you think it pays well, do you?" I teased as my head cocked just a tad.

"Yeah, I'd say it does. In fact, we gave notice hours after the explosion. It's not official until end of the month, but we are on leave until then," offered Jake earnestly.

With piqued interest, my brow raised, I asked, "Did Freddy negotiate these terms?"

Jake and Steve laughed simultaneously. "No, Tom is the one giving orders on this."

They grow up quickly, don't they? "Well, who am I to argue with the man of the house? I guess I'd better touch base and see if there's anything else I need to be made aware of…pass me your burner phone," I smiled as I got up from the table. "Order some more wine, while I make a few phone calls. We have some work to do."

Jake handed me his phone and I left to go outside to talk in private. I noticed that Bethany was seated next to Steve and wondered if something had been "reunited" between them with this recent turn of events. If I was a betting woman, I'd also bet she suggested this idea to Tom. Just saying.

34

SEVEN

Hello

"HEY, JAKE, ANY NEWS?" he asked somberly.

You could feel the strain and worry in Tom's voice, not to mention it was 3 AM, his time. I imagined him laying in our bed with his long, muscular body, piercing blue eyes, his dark black hair, and a new thick beard. It was heartbreaking. Once again, he was left to wonder if his wife was alive or dead. I knew the feeling all too well after these recent events. My wonderful, supportive husband after all these years. We met via a "chance" encounter so many years ago. He's the balance to my life. He watches romantic movies; I watch videos on new weaponry or profiles of serial killers. He's all male despite the romantic movies, following collegiate and national sports and quoting stats with the best of them. He's smart, funny, and loyal to our family. He and our three children are my heaven on earth.

"It's me babe. It's me."

I felt the same raw emotions that he did: relief, despair, elation, gratitude, fragility, brokenness.

"What took you so long?" was all he could gather to get out, a small quiver in his voice.

"I'm so sorry, babe. I thought you were all dead," I slowly managed to respond with a trembling and sadness in my voice, but hurriedly added, "I saw the explosion, before I knew it, I was being rushed to a hospital, and saw on TV that there were no survivors. It was then reported that the explosion was outside Minot AFB, and I knew these were targeted attacks against anyone and everyone I loved and cared for. I was beside myself with grief, thinking I'd lost you, the kids, my parents, Bethany and Freddy – all in a matter of minutes. I lost it."

The only thing that came to mind was Coolio's *Gangster of Death*…"*As I was walk through the valley of the shadow of death, I take a look of my life and realize there's nothin' left…*".

"Oh God, babe, I'm so sorry. I had no idea. I can't imagine how you dealt with that all alone. I'm surprised you didn't clue in on the fact I had taken items from the hotel room after the attack. That's not like you."

"Yeah, well, in my defense, I overlooked that due to head and psychological trauma. Obviously, I didn't handle this too well. I jumped on a plane and was about to start a world-wide *Rambo.*"

Tom had a slight chuckle over that thought, and the trepidation finally dropped. "I wouldn't have expected anything less, and if anything ever does happen to us, feel free to burn them all to the ground."

"Like you have to tell me that. I got your back, baby. God, I'm so glad to hear your voice. I just can't function right without you." We both just sat on the line to let it all sink in. *Breathe in, breathe out.* "So, I see you've been negotiating some new personnel for us…"

"Well, yeah…" He lightly stammered, and was trying to play lighthearted. "I felt we needed to go in a new direction and… well, hell, Matti, I just want to protect our family. You've been trained for this. I'm just learning. I can't go through this scenario again."

This poor man. Consider everything I have put him through for the sake of national security. "I think it was a smart move, and one we should have considered a long time ago."

"Have you talked to Freddy yet?" he inquired.

"He's my next call. I just found out thirty minutes ago that you all were alive. It's been a hell of a morning. I can't tell you how relieved I was to see Bethany and the boys. I just wish it was you."

"Ditto, babe."

"Did you just Patrick Swayze me?" I teased.

"Nah, not intentionally." He laughed for the first time. "What's next?

"I need to check on my parents, too, but will wait until it's after 8 AM their time. I don't mind waking Freddy." I had a rather large grin as I stated that last sentence. "How are the kids taking all of this?"

"They'll be glad when they get to talk to Momma finally, but other than that, they have been more resilient that I have. Damn, it's disheartening at times. I feel like such a puss, sometimes, compared to them."

"Ha, I know what you mean. I've blacked out two times over the last week. I'll never hear then end of it from Jake and Steve."

"You did? Why do I always miss out on all the fun? I bet you are glad Bethany is there. I just wish I was," Tom continued.

"Me too, love, but I'm glad you are there with the kids while we figure out the next moves."

"Since you are in Ravello, I'm assuming you've seen Aldo by now. Is he partaking in these so-called next moves?"

"Yes, and we have some new allies, too, that I need to fill you in on. We will need to hammer out some specifics, but just as John Rambo said…*They drew first blood, not me.*"

"Oh lord. Allies, huh? I can only imagine." And with that, he had a more robust laugh.

EIGHT

P.O.I

"I SHOULDN'T BE SURPRISED that you'd choose to call at this hour," Freddy answered on the first ring.

Freddy was just a tad shorter than my husband, probably more around 6'3. His hair was now gray, but he had a relatively toned body for his age. I pictured him being in bed right now, with rumpled sheets and a leftover glass of scotch.

"I can see now where I get the warm and fuzzy side from…how about I start with…hello, Father, I'm alive." I can say confidently that I have never called Freddy "father" in my lifetime. I only recently found out he was my father, and as far as I was concerned, he was still my commander, first. Maybe that would change later? Who knows?

"Touché, Matti. You were never one to be confused with beating around the bush, so to speak. I'm glad you are ok. How are you holding up?" he asked sincerely.

"Well, considering the last ninety-six hours when I thought my whole family, extended family, and friends had been assassinated, I'm doing better now." No point to belabor the point. "We can get into small talk later. The first item of business is: did you figure out how we were tracked, despite being off grid for the last month?"

"Unfortunately, yes. When I was abducted near the Pentagon,

when you were in midst of your FUBAR mission. They had me holed up in an abandoned barn for hours. I did a full sweep of my house, cars, and offices when it was all over. Nothing was found. The only thing I didn't sweep was the actual clothes I was wearing that day. They planted it in the sole of my Testoni Italian men's dress shoes. I had them on when we met at the restaurant."

"Fucking Rogers. US citizens have every reason to be wary of any agency that leads the overall clearance and surveillance of citizens under the pretense of protection. I should have put a bullet in his fat head when I had the chance," I said, exasperated.

"In hindsight, that probably would have been a better option, but we needed to follow him and see his connections. As you've witnessed, this tangled web has many players."

"It's time to take down this web, player by player, starting with Rogers. What do have on his associates? Namely, Russia and China."

"The Prime Minister, Damien Azrail, is definitely affiliated with Rogers," Freddy started.

I've always been fascinated by name origins. In this case, Damien equals "one who tames others" and Azrail means "the angel of death." Just great. First: in this day in age, what twisted person names any kid Damien? I mean, really. No wonder he's screwed up. Remember the little kid's eyes who played in the movie *Omen?* Yeah, still creeps me out.

"The Prime Minister is appointed by the President and confirmed by the State, so is he party to this as well?" I inquired.

"No concrete evidence to verify, but he's on a short leash, and let's not forget who succeeds the president if they die or are incapacitated."

"That would be the angel of death, Azrail."

"Bingo," Freddy chimed.

"What's the status of China?"

"The Director of NSC is Wang Shaung Fu."

The National Supervisory Committee is essentially our version of the Supreme Court. It was established during the first term of the Xi Jingping era as the highest anti-corruption agency for the People's Republic of China. It wasn't until late 2016 that new initiatives were implemented to stop the arbitrary exercise of power. This timing happens to coincide with the demise of high-level personnel on our home front. NSC would also have the final say in any issues arising from the National Medical Products Administration, aka our version of FDA.

I don't believe in coincidences.

Wang = King

Shaung = double

Fu = luck

"Does he have a sister or brother?" I probed.

In the 1980s, China implemented their draconian law of "one-child" to prevent overpopulation and to deal with an aging population. Exceptions to the rule were allowed for couples in agriculture, or if a parent's first child was disabled. In those cases, they could try for another. Theoretically, if a couple had twins, they would not be penalized if they had only one birth per family. Of course, this opened a loophole for fertility treatments. By breaking the policy, the second child would not receive a household register, which is equivalent to our social security number. They wouldn't be able to attend schools or receive insurance, and are known as "shadow children."

"He had a twin sister. It is believed the parents smothered her before she turned one, despite the official death record of sudden infant death syndrome."

"Ok, so, we have the Angel of Death and a tormented twin on a mission to change the world. What have we found out about the missing scientists?"

"Still MIA. It would require some serious calculated collaboration to keep seven scientists hidden from multiple international agencies looking for them," Freddy acknowledged.

"There's 7.5 billion people in this world. I think you can hide 7 people. Or they may be dead already, but I doubt it. I'd say they have a lot of collaboration between Rodgers and Williams, and we need verification on whether CIA Directors Sedlin and Long are involved, as well. I don't feel that they are. They seem pretty inept, if you ask me, but that's all the more reason why they could be used or abused in this situation."

"Our pals in the Middle East have been awfully quiet," he continued.

"Too quiet."

"What if…" Freddy started, but I cut him off.

"Freddy, there are no 'what ifs' for me, at this point. They collaborated to assassinate my entire family. You included. Let's not forget that. I'm reasonable until provoked. I won't get all the parties involved, but I will take the heads out—the ones responsible for my personal attack. We'll let the chips lie after that, so to speak, and will see what we need to do afterwards."

"There're global ramifications to that, Matti. You can't just go out there and take them all out."

"Oh yeah? Watch me."

And I considered the Muse lyrics in my head, *Psycho… "I'm going to break you. I'm going to make you. A fucking psycho…"*

NINE

Regroup

WHEN I RETURNED TO THE GANG, they were three bottles deep in conversation. I noticed Bethany was sitting just a tad bit closer to Steve. What an actress! I couldn't wait to give her grief on this. I mean, after all, what are best friends for?

"How did it go?" Bethany asked sincerely as I approached the table.

"Good. I got a hold of both Tom and Freddy. Looks like I'm missing out on a party, here."

"We're celebrating our new job. Best part? We charged everything to your room boss." Steve smiled as he raised a glass in the air.

"Please, shoot me now." I proceeded, "We may need to revisit that negotiation, but let's save it for later. We have some planning to do." I poured myself a glass to join them and we hoisted the glasses to toast, "to ending this once and for all."

I turned to Bethany and asked what transport she'd obtained.

"Oh, you're going to really like this one. I secured a Gulfstream G650ER for transport."

"Please tell me that we didn't buy it, but made other arrangements."

"My, my, how picky. Mind you, I didn't have a lot of time to shop around, but no, "we" did not buy, per say," Bethany retorted.

"You might want to clarify 'we'…did any singular pronoun of any one person we know purchase this craft?"

"No, no, it's not like that. We—being any of us in this room, nor Tom and Freddy—did not purchase this craft. Think of it more as an extended lease with benefits," she continued awkwardly, trying to avoid the real answer.

With any luxury item, there are requirements to ensure that the value is not diminished before the expiration of said item. For a Gulf Stream, you would have minimum hours you would need to purchase in each period at an escalating rate for shorter durations.

"How extended? Wait, doesn't Ralph Lauren own one of these?" I inquired.

"I'm not sure, but I think he does. We needed transport, regardless, so this should accommodate us nicely for the next year."

What an actress she is. Like she doesn't know if he owns one. Bethany was considered an esteemed pilot and top consultant for many major airlines and had deep ties in the navigation world. Hell, she could have borrowed one from Lauren, Bill Gates, or Tiger Woods, for that matter. She obviously wanted to commandeer this one. "Ok, one year. Don't you think it would have been a lot simpler to just say that?"

"Well, plus or minus a bit, but yeah, that's about it."

"At this point, I don't want to know," I professed, while doing mental calculations of the cost in my head.

Steve interrupted teasingly, "Do we need to be here for this conversation?" It was his feeble attempt to change the subject and move on.

These little scoundrels. I'm betting Steve gave her the suggestion. If I hadn't thought she was murdered, just days before,

I would have probed more.

"Well, regardless, it's a good thing. You're going to need to drop me off, drop off the boys, then head back stateside to meet up with Freddy, Tom, and the kids."

"When we are leaving?" asked Jake.

"Well, since our pilot has been drinking, it won't be today. Tomorrow at 9 am we need to be wheels up."

"That leaves us the whole day. What did you have in mind?" Steve asked excitedly.

"I need help loading some things I left here, and we will need to obtain them by boat. Looks like we have a fun day ahead of us, on the water."

"Oh, God, no. I can't take the three of you on a boat singing your tone-deaf tunes." Bethany was already getting up and walking away with her palm facing us in the air.

"Now, B, that's not right. I thought you were dead just days ago, and now you want to refuse time with me? I'm hurt, truly."

"Shut it, woman," she said, smiling. "What all are we procuring?"

"Just a small arsenal. You'll need to transport some of these personal items back for me for storage."

Jake and Steve pushed their chairs back and got up from the table as well. Jake looked at me and simply said, "John?"

"Oh yes, that would be a perfect start," I said, and I started humming Jon Bon Jovi's *It's My Life.*

"I have not had enough to drink to endure this. This boat had better be stocked," Bethany was heard to say as she paced herself in front of us.

Without missing a beat, the boys and I chimed in unison: "*It's my life, it's now or never…*"

TEN

Vroom Vroom

THE GANG HAD A PRODUCTIVE TIME on the boat, allowing us to secure my personal items and discuss and theorize next steps. It was time to divide and conquer.

The plane was loaded. Bethany would be dropping me off first, before she and the boys proceeded.

"You ready for this?" she asked as I was about to disembark.

I looked at each of them. They were my family. "I can't thank you enough for everything you have done for me and my family over the years. I love you guys."

"Don't go getting soft on us. It's our pleasure to serve," Jake offered.

"I don't know what you are talking about. I was just here for the booze," Steve added with his disheveled grin.

I gave both boys a hug and then Bethany walked me down the ramp. She turned to me and said, "Your hair looks good in its natural color. Glad to see you go au natural. You look similar to Blake Lively in that *A Simple Favor* movie."

"I'm good with that. Of course, I'd kick all of their asses," I teased.

"Well, that's obviously a given."

"True…For this part, Scotti Worthington is now done, and Matti

Baker makes her first return appearance from the dead."

She looked at me, taking it all on. Finally, she said, "Well, ok, I'll see you when I see you."

"If all goes to plan, you'll see me in less than ten days. No need to go cryptic on me and give us bad mojo, now."

Her eyes glistened as she pulled me closer to wrap her arms around me. "Take care of yourself. I can't lose you again."

"I was about to say the same thing. It's a good thing this plane can go Mach .85. You need to hightail it out of here so we can time these efforts. I'm counting on you, as always."

"Technically, I think it can go Mach .90. Don't worry, we'll test it out to make sure," she added, while letting go of the embrace.

"Love you, B," I stated as I started to walk off. I was five feet away when I turned around and said, "Hey, when I get back, I want to hear all about you sleeping with Steve again."

"What the hell! How do you always know these things?" she asked incredulously with her hands in the air.

She could hear me laughing as I continued walking towards the gate, waving a good-bye with my hand in the air.

Aldo was there, waiting on my arrival in a sleek, black Mercedes AMG G63. Unlike the typical sedans that I was accustomed to him driving, this one was a boxy SUV that looked like a tank.

"Bonjourno, Aldo. Sweet ride. What's the occasion?"

"Miss Matti, we figured we needed some added protection just in case. You have a habit of people wanting you dead."

"Hmm. Good point, thanks. Is everything on schedule?"

"Yes, they are expecting our arrival and your special modifications have been installed."

"Isn't it amazing what money can do?" I responded.

Aldo just smirked knowingly. "Yes, it does have a profound impact, doesn't it?"

We drove to Maranello, Italy, which was just under a two-hour drive from the airport. On the way, we discussed provisioning and each party's involvement in the next steps. Again, I reiterated that timing would be crucial and paramount for success.

Maranello is a quaint Italian town, its main claim to fame being the headquarters for Ferrari and the Formula One racing team. I had requested a special edition and was looking forward to the seeing my newest purchase, the Ferrari 812 Superfast.

The redesigned 812 has a dual clutch transmission, 789hp, and can propel you from 0-60mph in 2.9 seconds with top speeds over 211mph. The 812 is second fastest vehicle they produce, just behind the LaFerrari. The price tag is roughly $350,000 before the custom moderations I made, which brought the total to just over $500,000.

I selected this vehicle for three reasons. One, it's gorgeous. Two, its maneuverability and speed, which I would need. Third, and most important: it had to be in a certain price range. (Plus, LaFerrari costs about $2.2 million before alterations, and couldn't be obtained in such short request period. But, believe me, I tried.)

Our government has a long history of monitoring phone and online communications as well as credit card transactions. The stated purpose of this monitoring was to thwart terrorism so they could identify if someone had purchased bomb ingredients or was moving funds illicitly. I was counting on the NSA actually doing their job, today. NSA works with credit cards companies, and red flags are sent when items or prices hit certain levels. I was about to implement this, which would send it promptly to Rodgers and William's attention.

By collecting data at the processor level, you can technically track a purchase down to the person. NSA could contact the bank issuing the credit card to obtain the name of the individual, in such an event. I had one better. Due to the nature of my business as a contractor, I was using a government-issued credit card with an open line of credit, thus eliminating the need for NSA to contact a third party to verify the account holder, as it would show that it was issued to Matti Baker. Ta da. *"Here's Johnny."* I was also counting on my card not being deactivated, but I could procure my own card if necessary. It would just add an additional step.

The 812 was brought out to the parking lot in a brilliant "grigio silverstone" color, aka dark grey. I really preferred the "nero" or black, but I had to admit this was a stunning beast. The white leather was pristine, and just once in your life, you need a car that starts with a "launch" button. The back was stripped and modified to fit my necessary carry-on, and nothing outside of a rocket launcher was going to penetrate it.

"Thank you for accommodating my requests so quickly," I said to Stefano, the day manager, as I continued to check out the vehicle. I'm sure he was vacillating between hoping this would not come back to him personally to being excited at what they were able to accomplish.

"We are ready to process payment when you are, Ms. Baker," he said as he handed over a remote terminal for me to enter my information.

Aldo opened the back and put my case in there, while dropping a backpack in the passenger seat. "We're ready when you are, dear child," he said as he extended his hand to shake mine and kissed me on each cheek.

I pressed the last button to submit and handed it back to Stefano. "It's been a pleasure, gentlemen. You may want to stand back now.

I have a clock to beat." And with that, I closed the door and pressed 'launch.'

ELEVEN

Catch me if you can

TIME MANAGEMENT IS ESSENTIAL to any successful venture and was something I obsessed about continually. Milliseconds could make or break a mission.

Italy was experiencing an unusually warm climate for this time of year. I drove off from the dealership anticipating how much time I had before satellite surveillance on me would be ordered. The time of purchase in Italy, minus seven hours, put the US time at 6 AM when the first alert would go off. I was hoping to buy a little leeway time by having the alert hit in the early morning hours. Nothing like being woken and having to scramble. Fuck you, Rogers. If it's left to me, he wouldn't have a decent night's sleep again before he perished. I wonder if he realized that this morning?

One of the things you will notice when traveling in Italy, in comparison to the US, is the lack of police vehicles on the highway. Police do not bother with speed enforcement. Italy uses cameras and will cite drivers, via license plates, who travel faster than ten percent over the allotted speed limit. First, the speed limit is higher than we are accustomed to, and locals pretty much abide by the rules, understanding the mafia enforcement and its implications. Second, it could take months for violations to be tracked down to foreigners due to car rentals, etc. Visitors are often stumped when they receive tickets seven months to a year after they visited the country. The moral decision whether to pay or not to pay in a country you'll likely never visit again is an individual assessment. These license plate readers submit to a central database, and the US would be requesting access based on my recent purchase. When you want to catch a fat mouse, you have to dangle a few crumbs.

I had a three-hour drive to reach my new destination and was heading south-west to the town of Carrara. Carrara has produced marble from its mountainside since the time of Ancient Rome. In fact, today it produces more marble than any place on earth. Fascinating to think that huge marble slabs from here were escorted to Rome centuries ago. Intense religious disputes followed, with Carrara becoming foundation of anarchy among the quarry workers. Today, it remains a hotbed of debate, with marble being exported around the world and the demolition of the mountainside conflicting with the preservation of Italy.

As I cruised the gorgeous terrain to Carrara, Freddy called to give me a status update.

"Hope you are making good time. We have good news and news neither of us was expecting."

"Dear Jesus, please tell me the good news first."

"Well, you wanted to bring the fight to you, and that's going to be the case. In fact, sooner than you thought."

"Pray tell."

"Rodgers departed on a flight last night to Afghanistan. After the notification of your potential "rebirth," he was rerouted to Ramstein AFB and has been ordered by Williams to track you down and confirm your demise himself."

In Afghanistan you have the Taliban, but during recent events there, Hezbollah had claimed responsibility. Hezbollah was founded by Iran to harass Israel, but has grown substantially in size. Their main objective was to fight American and Israeli imperialism. Simply put, they waged war on iconic locations for maximum fear and maximum economic damage. Bad dudes, very bad dudes. The fact that Rodgers was being directed to go after me versus continuing there spoke volumes.

Ramstein is in Kaiserslautern, Germany, and is the only main NATO command with a state-of-the art facility built originally to monitor the Soviet Union that now intermingles directly with the Pentagon, USAFE bases, and Supreme Headquarters Allied Powers Europe.

"Well, that's very good news, indeed. I had calculated another day before it came to fruition, but that just speeds up the timeline for me. The visit to Afghanistan could be coincidental, or another reason to suspect their involvement, as well. What will he be flying?"

"Well, that's the not so good news. He'll be coming to you on a C-40B with normal crew."

The C-40 is a simpler version of Airforce One. It's a luxury skybox passenger transport used to transport senior military and top government leaders with a crew of ten. Designed by Boeing and modeled after the 737, communications are the supreme feature on board, allowing commanders to conduct business anywhere. This was an added plus for us, on this venture, but also an added challenge, as we would need to crack one of the most secure networks on the airwaves. Nothing could ever just be easy, could it?

As I was processing what Freddy just mentioned, he said, "I think we need to give them a reason to abandon ship, like in the *Hunt for Red October*, or prepare to pull a *U-571.*"

"Interesting, but we don't have enough time allotted to board under disguise. It looks like we'll have to incite them to jump. A change to our original plan, but I think it will work out better. How is surveillance on Williams?"

"We're monitoring everything on her. The irony is that we're monitoring people who are feverishly trying to locate us," he said matter-of-factly.

"Well, let's make sure this time we stay one step ahead. You have new shoes on today, right?" I said mockingly.

Silence. *I guess it was too soon for that.*

I quickly proceeded, "Ok, keep me updated. I'll need transport myself after this, and let's make sure the boys in blue are taken care of, after this all goes down."

"That's a lot of targets you must quickly identify in a short amount of time," Freddy offered with concern.

"Not really. It's a last-minute unscheduled flight. Most likely only one of them will be wearing a business suit, and he'll be the priority first off. Fly, Fight, Win. I'll be 'aiming high', as they like to say."

TWELVE

Payback

TIC. TOCK. It all boils down to timing. I had to stay ahead to get to my destination, while allowing enough time for them to locate me, but not catch me per say…as there would be no "catching" in this case.

I flew in this car. It was incredible. Maneuvered like it was on rails, as Richard Gere said in *Pretty Woman*. My three-hour trip was reduced significantly due my speed, so I was in position and calculated I had twenty minutes to get a showdown that was coming a day earlier. Why waste time, right? I toggled through some music and was going back and forth between on Tracy Chapman's *Fast Car* ("…*You got a fast car and I got a plan to get us out of here…*") and Def Leppard's *Rocket* ("…*Take a rocket, we just gotta fly, I can take you through the center of the dark...*"). Both were just right to set the mood.

I called Tom and Bethany. "Hey, it's almost go time. You set?"

Tom answered first. "I've been working frantically, but have eyes on you now, while B hacked into their online system and set up the malware. How are you doing on your end?"

"Cool as a cucumber. I'm in position and ready for whatever option plays out. It's a shame we won't be able to keep this car when it's all over."

"There's really something wrong with you, when you are more concerned about a damn car, at this juncture. By the way, can we just acknowledge for a moment what a feat it is to hack into this system? I should be a superhero," Bethany piped in.

"Jealousy is not becoming on you, B. And give yourself an obligatory pat on the back, if you must," I teased back.

"Just stay focused, wench."

"Love you, too. I'll switch over once this all starts. Tom, I.." and I paused for just a second. "We got this, baby. I love you so."

"Just get your ass home so we can continue our tradition," he commanded.

"Gross. I don't want to hear about that," Bethany admonished.

"The damn wine, B. Potty brain. Jesus." I laughed as I hung up.

Never had I done this on a previous mission, but I quickly called the kids. After recent events, I felt compelled. I called Mary's phone, as I knew she always had it on, and she answered on the first ring. "Hey, Momma."

"Hey, baby, what are you all doing? Are the boys with you?"

"Yeah, they are right here. We have a few minutes left before we report back to Ainsworth. You know, he can be a bit of a killjoy at times," she said incredulously.

"Ha, that's his job, sweetheart. Pay attention, he's a smart man. Put me on speaker phone so the boys can hear me."

We talked for a few minutes, catching up, and then I was pinged on my new Patek Phillipe watch. "Loves, I have to go now, but Momma loves you so. I'll see you soon, babies."

"Love you, Mom," Matthew said.

"I'll remind the others I'm your favorite after we hang up," Mark teased. "Go kick some butt, Mom."

With that, it was showtime.

The C-40B would be in range soon, and would have the same satellite imaging on me. It was almost time to see if we were going with Option 1, or Option 2.

I was situated at the bottom of the 2,000-foot mountain range which spiraled into one lane climb to reach the top. Camouflaged in the white and grey ashes of the mountain, I had the perfect cover. Thank God I didn't get the black car, but it really wouldn't matter, as this car would be covered in soot within seconds of me careening up the mountainside at lightning-fast speeds. *I feel the need, the need for speed.*

I had Tom and Bethany on bluetooth. "Let's do this."

"They have tracking on you, but are not in range for any short-range limited assault, yet. You do realize we are counting on this being more of a passenger plane that's not equipped for much else, based on last minute flight changes?" Bethany said.

"If you do your job right, it shouldn't matter..." I left it hanging.

"Shut it. On my count, get going...3,2,1...go."

With that, I launched that damn car and said a little Hail Mary as I careened up the road at what felt like rocket speeds.

Now, here's where it got tricky. I had to go at speeds fast enough that they couldn't IED me if they had anything, while the rising dust swirls would be helping my cover but also made it difficult to drive at the speeds I was going, with almost zero visibility. I'd had extra features added to the car to help navigate that dilemma. The suspension lifting system was not a standard option, but an additional option I had added. I had only so much time to make it to the top, where Aldo had left me a little present. Bless that man.

"Tom, please tell me you have audio to broadcast for us."

"Coming on now," he said as I heard the crew in the cockpit and the joining parties on audio. From all accounts, it sounded like we had Williams on call and an unidentified top Air Force official, Rodgers, and a few others in a conference room.

"Is that her? Can we confirm it's her? It doesn't look like her. More importantly, where is this woman going? This makes no sense," Rodgers stammered.

'Sir, the best we can assess is that the woman is determined to make it to the top the top of the mountain," a voice from the room stated.

"No shit, I can assess that myself."

"This makes no sense. What short-range missiles are on board?" Williams barked.

"Ma'am, our orders are to watch and observe, and to communicate location. We are in Italy's air space and it would be a violation of our treaty, not to mention the severe economic and financial impact of a direct hit to their marble mountain," he said calmly but authoritatively.

For the next fifteen seconds, you could hear them bickering back and forth about whose authority took precedence, and the ramifications of their actions. All this did was allow me to advance up without any unnecessary altercations or modifications.

At 2,000 feet, on a normal straight flat road, if you were driving 100 mph, you travel 146.67 feet per second. Unfortunately for me, this was not a flat road, and I had 90-degree turns roughly every 250 feet.

"Then get close enough where we can open a door and personally shoot this woman. I don't care what you do, Officer, but she is not to get off that mountain top," Rodgers could be heard screaming.

Over the audio, you could hear from the cockpit, "Gentlemen, we may have a problem. We have visual imaging not detected by satellite. It appears to be a large covered mass at the top of mountain range. It looks like military-grade camouflage netting. Please advise."

"It's a trap. Who knows what is stored up there? You need to stop her NOW! This is a matter of national security!" exclaimed Williams.

The pilots responded, "The woman is reaching the unknown structure and pulling the camouflage off.

"Good lord, it looks like an old Howitzer," the pilot said anxiously.

"Kill that bitch before she kills us!" threatened Rodgers.

Just then, I relayed to Bethany, "Now."

With a few keystrokes, the next thing the pilots were overheard to say on intercom was, "Please be advised, we have a breach and a slow shutdown of the main engine. Trying to get it back on."

"That goddamn bitch is going to kill us all. We are right above her. Kill her now!" Rodgers continued to bark.

"Sir, we have our orders, and we need to ensure our own safety first, at this point."

"We're all going to be dead! Fuck your orders, I'll do it myself."

The pilots came back on the intercom feverishly speaking. "We have failure in our second engine. We'll take steps to evacuate and we will attempt to get engines back on, and if not, hopefully we'll make it to the Mediterranean."

Sheer fucking pandemonium. *Fuck you, Rodgers. You should have made sure I was dead at the restaurant, you chicken shit piece of crap.*

As personnel scrambled for parachutes and to open doors, I was in the back of my car, setting up.

Since Rodgers was the highest priority personnel on flight, they would ensure he was escorted off first.

"Bethany, get ready. I'll need to verify and give you a go."

It took a bit longer than I had expected, but it's hard to get people to willingly jump out of plane, especially narcissistic egomaniacs.

First person out, followed by second. I relayed, "Confirmed. Go!"

THIRTEEN

Dead Man (not) Walking

BETHANY HAD BOTH ENGINES BACK and operating just before it was necessary for any additional personnel to jump. It's all about timing.

Rodgers pulled his parachute. The second person was heading east to the opposite side of the mountain, due to winds. Rodgers was gliding over to the west. At one point, I thought he might be heading closer to me, but winds were shifting, and I couldn't wait any longer.

Now it was time for me to finish this charade.

One of the little jewels I picked up in Ravello was a McMillan TAC-50 sniper rifle, which has the longest recorded kill range, of over 3,450 meters. Although I wanted to riddle his body with bullets, I realized I didn't need to. I just needed two simple shots. No, not to the head, that would be too easy...through his chute. I pulled the trigger for the first shot and damn it if my fucked-up index finger didn't mess my timing up. It was throbbing again. I used my middle finger, which worked just fine, for the next two shots. Specifically, I shot the break line and riser chords, which I tore through precisely.

He would be free falling from just under 10,000 feet. On average, you fall 200 feet per second in a sky dive, so freefall would be roughly thirty seconds. Thirty seconds to wonder what he did wrong. How had this happened? It had to be me. Why didn't he kill me when he had a chance?

Damn, the winds were picking up at this altitude. I quickly loaded "Millie" back in and pressed 'launch.' I followed his freefall, and could picture his eyes wide with terror as he hit the mountain and started to roll (well, hit) repeatedly down. Damn, that had to hurt. I used my middle finger again, in a final salute.

The last thing probably going through his mind was wondering why he gave a heads up at the restaurant and the f'in bitch didn't miss the shot this time. I couldn't hear, but knew he would be screaming. I always enjoyed when Kevin Costner, who played Eliot Ness in *The Untouchables,* said, *"Did he sound anything like that?"*

One down.

How could this have happened? Just as I had been blinded at the restaurant, relying on only visual, so I used the same theory on them.

First thing they should have asked was why would I purchase a Ferrari to alert them to my presence? Puh-please, like I'm really that stupid. (I do love this car, though.)

Next, after driving hours through every known camera to locate 'the blonde woman', what was my escape route, going up a marble mountain? I predicted they wouldn't be authorized to shoot me over Italian air space, nor equipped. Did they think I was going to do a Tom Cruise and paraglide off it? I mean, I guess I could have.

Then, why would a Howitzer cannon be on top of said mountain in Italy? Granted, the Howitzer was originally built to hit high trajectories with a steep angle descent, but here on this marble mountain? Come on, people, think! Had they looked closer, they would have noticed it was a modified tractor that was used to move these large slabs of marble. Aldo graciously added a short barrel to mimic a real cannon. When I took the camouflage off, their eyes saw what they perceived based on the panicked conversation of a room of people who had no visual.

Let's not forget Bethany's part. To sum it up simply, the problem with technology is that it's digital. It's there or it isn't. When you have older planes retrofitted for today's world, you are trusting modifications. Ever notice that old laundry machines last for decades, but new ones only last a few years? Why is that? When they are digital, they are prone to glitches, and one little glitch stops the whole thing. Bethany did an *Independence Day* and gave them a little virus so they would shut off their seemingly malfunctioning engines. We knew they'd have to follow protocol, after that.

Oh, and let's not forget my hubby. Tom did a great job in making sure we could hear all their communications. This allowed us to play on their fears. I needed to remember all that Tom did when we got together to celebrate…if you know what I mean. Hubba, hubba.

Freddy had been patched in from the start, and was now asking my ETA.

"I'm driving as fast as I can."

"Aldo is meeting you with your new transport. We have help from our friends in locating and returning the other jumper. Thanks to Tom, the C-40 had communications permanently cut off with Williams, and the pilots were ordered to return to Ramstein. It's doubtful they will be able to confirm that Rogers's chords were shot, after that fall, so we could have plausible deniability, since they would all confirm that they saw a blonde woman and, technically, they still can't confirm it's you—just that someone used your government-issued card," Freddy continued.

"Is it really necessary to give this car up? It's not like the American government can take it back, plus I haven't had it long enough to even name it."

"I got a name. How about 'Rose?'" Bethany piped in.

"You mean the Testarosa from *Gone in Sixty Seconds*? It's a good thing you are overseas. Just saying. How about that track from Ice Cube, Roll All Day? "*... Now we could roll all day, if I could ride all night, I got a full tank of unleaded, I got a full tank of unleaded...*"

Freddy disconnected. I heard Tom laughing in the background.

FOURTEEN

Next please

ALL GOOD THINGS MUST COME TO AN END. And with that, I tearfully said good-bye to the 812 and told Aldo to consider this as partial payment for his services. Let's just say he didn't put up a fight.

My new traveling buddy was here to board with me. Bessum and I boarded a private charter and were headed to Mother Russia…Moscow.

Traveling between different time zones and countries, I always took the liberty of sleeping on planes. It's unnerving to others for some reason—I guess due to the nature of our business—but, hey, I gotta sleep for maximum performance, and had no issues closing my eyes before the plane took off.

Bes and Lily were a little apprehensive originally about their participation when they heard that my family, indeed, had not been murdered, but also were more convinced as they understood that the threat was real. They must have watched *Untouchables,* too, as they believed, *"Never stop fighting 'til the fight is done."* God love them.

Azrail worked in Moscow, but his country estate was roughly forty-five minutes away in the Odintsovsky District 9. Try to say that five times real fast. Luckily, Bes was fluent in Russian, as mine needed some work. With all this technology, I was surprised there was no real-time application that translates verbal and written language. It would be a gold mine. I need to investigate this idea for investment opportunities.

Our attire for a traveling couple was spot on. We had on enough fur to have PETA protest us for life, but more importantly, this allowed us to conceal our weapons for this quick turnaround. Bes brought another needed accessory, his little pug pooch, appropriately named…Dimples.

Personally, I can't say I'm a fan of small dogs, but how could you not adore these wrinkly-faced, curly-tailed little bundles? So damn ugly, they are cute.

There's something comforting about routines. Ever notice that you watch the same movies over and over? Well, that's because our minds need the comfort of knowing what to expect. It's our mind's way of telling us we need to cry, laugh, or maybe just require some excitement.

The benefits of routines are that they allow you to utilize time efficiently, instill habits, and create structure. Detriments of routines? When you are a conniving world manipulator, they allow your opponents to target your punk ass.

Each day at noon, Azrail and his security team ventured to Suvorov Park to walk his Siberian husky. The park is majestic and borders the Moskva River. Large trees landscape the trail with limbs cascading over the water. It's the busiest time of the day, with the average person spending 1.5 hours in the park. Azrail was doing more than just walking his damn dog, it was his preferred location for transferring information. Russians hack and tamper with computers. They know better than to send a text, or post on Facebook. Just saying.

There was a brisk chill in the air as Bes and I walked arm-in-arm as a loving couple walking dear, sweet Dimples on the trail. Bes had his 'associates' provide us a detailed rundown of Azrail's walk. Apparently, Azrail was already under surveillance by the Albanian mafia, so my plea for help was just the icing they wanted on the cake. I took the military motto of "don't ask, don't tell."

We had determined our best location for elimination would be on a three-tier curved staircase that wouldn't allow for his security team to break away or have cover, except on the two landing areas between flights. The ineptness of the team was apparent, as I would never let my asset take this route.

The team walked two in front and two behind Azrail. We hoped no additional park goers would be in vicinity, but couldn't control that factor, since it was a busy public park.

We leisurely strolled and conversed for thirty minutes as Dimples made his way to our target destination. I was concerned the dog wouldn't last the additional time, with his little fat legs, but he sure was a trooper, and seemed to have energy to plow along. Made me miss my dogs. They would have loved this mission.

We expertly timed our approach to the top landing, as Azrail and his team were heading up from the bottom. There was one other park visitor with his back away from us, throwing the ball to his dog in the river. *(Damn, dude, that water is cold. Talk about animal cruelty.)*

The security detail in front yelled at us to stop and wait as they briskly started running up the stairs. (Mistake #1.)

Bessum screamed back, stating that he and his wife would be passing, and who are they to demand us to stop. Truthfully, I had no idea what the hell he was saying or what was being exchanged. Damn, my Russian really sucked, now. I used to be more fluent. Dimples was now barking up a storm, lending Azrail's husky to take defensive actions, pulling harder on the leash to commandeer him up the stairs.

As the two security ran up with revolvers out, we were 10 steps down from the top landing, and they were upon us still screaming in mother tongue to back up. (Mistake #2.) With nowhere to go, with railings on each side, Azrail and the other two security agents were now approaching the second landing, and we needed to act before they reached cover.

Bes let go of Dimples and shot the first two, but not before he was hit in the shoulder. Luckily, his bulletproof vest took the blunt of it.

While Bes had the first team, I took out the bottom two and the dog, who was climbing rapidly.

We didn't kill the dog. We shot all of them with my infamous dart concoction. Normally, I prep these darts with a lethal dosage, but this was more a 'slumber for hours' creation. Azrail would not realize that, though.

"That motherfucker shot at me. I think he needs more than just a dart!" Bes exclaimed as he kicked Azrail in the head.

"Save it for later, he's not our main target."

Azrail immediately put his hands in the air and begged for his life. Fat chance of that.

I peered down to the man throwing the ball to his dog, who quickly assessed the situation correctly and had already turned his back to run down the path.

I came face to face to Azrail. "Do you know who I am?"

He was wide-eyed, but calculating his options for survival. "Da."

"Good, speak English. I'm out of patience. Who is your US contact? Think quickly. I'm afraid I'm a little trigger-happy right now."

Pause.

"Answer the lady," Bes instructed.

"Williams," he answered.

"Who else is involved?"

"I'm not privy to all others. It is truth. We each just play our small roles."

One of the many things you learn in interrogation is to read the signs of when someone is lying. Their pitch of voice changes, the direction of their eyes, their stomach rumbles, yadda, yadda.

A bead of sweat was coming down his temple as he looked back and forth between Bes and me. I'm not sure who he feared more, but he'd just given us a sign. (Mistake #3.)

"Last chance, Azrail. Who else?" I stated calmly, as we were running out of time in a public park.

"I swear. I don't know. Don't kill me. I know nothing." he pleaded in broken English with that thick Russian accent.

"I won't kill you, but I can't give any promises about him," I said as I looked over to Bes.

Bes looked at me, his eyes started to gleam, and he asked, "You sure?"

In my best Drago impersonation, I shrugged my hands up in the air and said, "If he dies…he dies."

With that, Bes pulled out his Springfield and left a permanent mark.

Two down.

FIFTEEN

World Traveler

BES GRACIOUSLY ALLOWED ME to take his plane to the next location. Well, I guess you could say gracious, but I was paying for it, one way or another. I was meeting up with Lily in Beijing.

The timeline for completing activities would need to be escalated now, due to the demise of both Rodgers and Azrail. Williams would not be sitting idly, twiddling her thumbs while her top co-conspirators were being offed one by one.

You know what happens in Beijing (a lot) that no one talks about? Well, in their defense, no one talks about it in the US, either, but it's the good ole' prostitution industry. It's illegal, just like in the US, but it's everywhere. Where do you think the phrase 'happy ending" originated? Oy.

Remember the movie *Taken,* where the daughter was abducted (by the Albanians, mind you) and was being auctioned for a higher price since she was 'white'? There's over twenty-one million people in Beijing. Unlike New York, where there is diversity of every race, creed and color…there's not so much in Beijing (or China, for that matter, with almost two billion people. That's with a "b," people). This isn't a racist comment, it's just is what it is.

With higher-level executives, some wives prefer prostitution over their husband's taking additional concubines, and generally the

Chinese are more compliant with prostitution then Westerners.

Now, you can find your normal run of the road prostitutes who give hand jobs, blow jobs, are street walkers, work karaoke bars, etc…or, for the more discriminating taste and for the right amount of money, you can go to a whole new level and direction.

Guess who didn't have a moral issue with this trade? Yeah, that would be Wang Shaung Fu. In English, the man has the word 'wang" as part of his name, for Christ's sake. He may as well just go by Dick. Ever meet any people named 'Dick' in the last three decades?

Wang also had a very well-known secret. It wasn't just prostitution he enjoyed, but he also preferred sadomasochism, where he could inflict pain and humiliation on others. Remember *Absolute Power*? Wang was the Director of the NSC, so who was going to tell him no?

I always said I feared women more than men when it came to devious ideas or retribution. Lily came up with this idea on her own. I was impressed, but also had a strong tingle in my head, like Elmer Fudd telling me …*be very, very, careful*.

Wang was a regular at the Intercontinental Hotel, giving 'luxury hotel' a whole new meaning. His executive suite had all the services of traditional luxury hotels, with his aides providing extra amenities you wouldn't find listed. *Fifty Shades* had nothing on this sick bastard.

Wang didn't have 'regulars', as many of them OD or went MIA after his visits. This left an opportunity for us to come in. What's better than sado with one, when you can have two, right?

Lily did not look her age. She could easily pass for thirty. Bitch. I was relying on Lily to bring us through this, as she was the one who'd posted her pic on the dark websites, soliciting the discriminating buyer. Her post said she was in town for specific date and time only and had the bonus of an American friend. Bait. Hook. Caught.

We entered the hotel and headed straight to the suite where his two-man security team inspected us and patted us down before we entered. One stayed outside, the other walked us in to be presented. Lily had brought a bag of goodies for the occasion, and had they inspected more thoroughly, they would have realized that a Ka Bar knife was in the large black dildo, and the cock ring with a pull-chord was for strangulation. Mind you, this was purchased, not self-assembled. There are some sick people in this world. I mean, really sick.

Wang was in his mid-fifties, roughly 5'7, an athletic build but slender, with black military buzz cut hair that made him appear stern. He was sitting by the balcony and did his best *True Lies* impersonation, sizing us up as he commanded for us to turn around so he could observe us from all sides. Enigma's *Principles of Lust* played in the background. Egad.

Lily was wearing a stunning Alexander McQueen rose-embellished, crystal rope halter gown that was backless. If I had to guess, it cost over ten grand. She brought for me an elegant, full-length Rosario one-shoulder, silver sequined gown with a high slit on the left side. Probably under two grand. I guess that solved who the dominatrix would be. I was still trying to recall the meaning of the acronym BSDM. I couldn't wait to laugh about this later with Tom.

Fortunately, we met with his approval and he gave the one finger flick with head lift to the security detail indicating he could leave the room.

"I have something for you to change into that is more appropriate for tonight's activities," he stated.

Thankfully, Lily took the lead and said she brought something he would approve of, and I could change after I watched this first session. Lucky me? He told her to change in front of him so he could watch and had me sit in the other side chair. Jesus Christ, he thinks he is Arnold Schwarzenegger in the movie. She slowly unhooked her dress to allow it to fall to the floor. I had the distinct impression that Lily had done this before, as she had no shame in her revealing her flawless body. She then reached into her bag of tricks and stepped into black leather front-less and ass-less chaps and donned it along with a black, menacing hood. What is wrong with people?

She grabbed his hand and led him to the bed. As she got closer to the bed, she then grabbed his head firmly and threw him onto it. That made him smile. So, he liked it rough. The next two minutes were painful in more ways than one. The hitting back and forth was shocking. I'm not sure she was role playing at this point. Visuals I could do without. Finally, she had him tied up. *Thank God.* I couldn't watch any longer.

I got up and made my way to the other room while checking for any cameras. The first security detail came towards me, asking what I needed, and I professed to needing help with unhooking my dress. He was a tall man, so I was mentally calculating what actions to take so not to cause too much of a loud commotion.

A strong elbow to the face broke his nose, but not before he got his hands around my neck to put me in a choke hold. It's simple math at this point. If I didn't do something quickly, his 6'4, 265-pound was going to overtake me and break my damn neck. With full force, I dropped to my knees while turning towards him, which forced him to bend over, as I had my full weight forcing him down to keep hold of me. I followed that by ramming my palm into his chin, which required him to let go of his grip to keep balance. The full-length dress prohibited me from standing up and kicking him in the head. I did jump up and grabbed the lead mantle décor to hit him, after that, forcing him off balance again while I took second hit to his head, knocking him out. Damn, I was winded. I relieved him of his .38 and promptly tied him up, taped his mouth shut, and administered a long-term sedative that I had stashed in my bra. I just hope the music covered any noise, as I expected Number Two to enter at any moment.

I swiftly made my way to the door to do the same thing to the other bloke. I had the .38 pointed at his head when I opened the door. His eyes glinted, assessing if he could take me, when I took the initiative to put the muzzle on his forehead and ask if he wanted to die here, now. He could do the math. I handed him a zip tie, and after he finished pulling it tight, I rammed a dart in his neck to finish it off. I then dragged his fat ass over to the other. I was pissed off that I was starting to sweat in this dress.

I think Lily was into her character a little too much. When I returned, she took off the hood and said, "Finally. Took your time. I didn't want to have to yank on his little wang any longer. I had the music blaring, hoping to cover up your actions."

Wang was in disbelief and yelled out to his team in Chinese to help him.

"No need to do that. They won't be coming," I said as I showed him the .38 I'd taken.

His menacing glare quickly dissolved as he understood the severity of the situation. As calmly as he could muster, he stated, more than asked, "What do you want? I am a very important man. You should know there will be deadly ramifications if anything happens to me."

"Shut it, psycho," Lily said as she slapped him hard across the face.

I think he thought we were still role-playing, as he was erect.

Sick, sick dude.

"Lily, please refrain, for the time being. I don't think he understands the situation correctly."

I pulled out another dart from my demi-bra lining and took off my black wig to reveal my true hair color.

"Do you know who I am?"

"That can't be. I received reports that you perished during the explosion. So, it was you. You were the one that killed Rogers and Azrail."

"Well, I guess you can't trust everything you read these days, huh? And yes, I took part in their 'departures'."

He laid there, tied up, naked, and motionless, understanding the finality of the situation.

"This dart has my special concoction. It will be slow and very, very painful. I will take my time and dismember you piece by piece and you will feel everything. You will tell me what I need to know."

"And what is my benefit, if I tell you?" he asked.

Ah, not so dumb after all. "It will be quick with this," I said, and I lifted the gun and pointed it towards him. He understood his situation completely, now.

"Which US agencies are involved, and what is your involvement? Take your time."

He started to talk. Outsiders fail to grasp the importance of Chinese honor ideology and practice. He would rather die than live, to save his honor. The same honor that allowed him to perform heinous acts. WTH.

The simple plan boiled down to modified eugenics. This is not a new tactic. During the Hitler regime, Hitler determined the Nordic race to be superior and eliminated biologically threatening genes from the population. Jews were purged, as they were viewed to be genetically unfit. Eugenics: the science of controlled breeding of desirable traits.

As he continued to talk, the magnitude was not lost that he honestly believed he was helping the world. History was trying to repeat itself, but with a twist. It was also apparent that each collaborating country was using this as an opportunity to individually aid their respective country by eliminating each other. It's like a sinister version of *Big Brother*—playing each other, telling lies, keeping secrets, forming alliances, voting people out...to be the only one standing at the end.

I think he appreciated the opportunity for a confession. He was not enraged, not fearful, but forthright. When pressed about the countries and agencies involved, he was adamant that, with recent turn of events over the last year, the coalition was smaller with the loss of leadership, that it was difficult identifying and recruiting new supporters, and that Williams remained the driving force.

When he was done talking, he bowed his head to his chest, as if to state that he was ready and had confided all the information that he possessed.

"One more question, Wang. Who has the scientists, then?"

His eyes widened as he reflected on the question, something he had not considered until now.

"They are in Afghanistan."

So, that explained why Rodgers was going there. Smoke and mirrors. We see what we want to see. And after being momentarily relieved that it was just Williams remaining, we both understood there were still other parties involved. US, Russia, China, and of course, our pals in The Middle East. Most likely others, as well. F' me.

Lily looked at me. "I can finish up here. You have a flight to catch."

The look in her eyes indicated that she would not shoot him first. I preferred to just put a bullet in his head than allow him to have any pleasure before his passing. I'm guessing she felt otherwise, since her husband would be incarcerated for the next forty years. Oy.

Three down...well, for all practical purposes.

SIXTEEN

Cave Dwellers

AFTER 9/11, THE US EMBARKED ON 'Operation Enduring Freedom" in Afghanistan. It's enduring, alright. We're still there today. It's the longest American war in history.

Trying to locate and drive the Taliban from power proved more complicated than originally anticipated. Their unconventional tactics— suicide attacks, turncoat killings, and guerilla raids— demonstrated that you can't reason or fight with insanity. Added to that, their terrain, with complex caves, proved difficult for locating the Taliban and Al-Qaeda. A few years back, the US dropped what would be considered the most powerful conventional bomb on an ISIS cave complex, annihilating everything within a thousand-yard radius. It's not rocket science, here—it's going to take more than one MOAB...just saying.

Bethany had dropped off Jake and Steve in Afghanistan before returning to the States. Who better to locate the seven missing scientists than Navy Seals, right?

Everyone always assumed the enemy was hiding in some massive underground, remote cave. That's the problem, when you assume. Not to mention that, technically, the only party looking for the scientists was us—and also technically, I still wasn't confirmed dead.

If you were a scientist, where would you be? In a cave or in a lab? There are over 117 hospitals that service Afghanistan, with the majority run by the Afghanistan government. We simply didn't have time to investigate them all. We scoured them all, including private hospitals, and quickly noticed only three that stood out. The US Army operates one in Bagram, NATO has one in Kabul, and the Red Cross has one in Kandahar. All three of these hospitals do not accommodate a lot of beds—but then, our scientists weren't there to treat patients. It was worth a shot. It wasn't imperative that we locate them before our next step, but it would prove beneficial if we did.

Tom hacked into Rodgers' itinerary and learned he was designated to fly into Kabul before he got rerouted, so the boys went there first. Big goose egg.

Bagram is roughly an hour and a half drive from Kabul, and Kandahar is over eight hours. Rock, paper, scissors. They went to Bagram first. Rodgers would have a reason to visit here, but once again it was a big nada.

We were hedging bets and running out of time. Jake relayed, "Matti, we're not sure we want to continue, at this point. This last location has been destroyed and rebuilt. It holds under thirty staff members and seems to lack the facilities and resources they would need."

"What else do we have on this?" I asked.

"They receive over 70% of their funding from the International Committee of the Red Cross."

"Who built it?"

There was a pause while he looked before he said, "I got it up now...They got aid from China."

"Get your asses to Kandahar. I'm betting they are storing more than just blood there. Keep me updated, but I'll make sure we have room for the ride home if we have additional guests."

The American Red Cross was established to provide emergency assistance in disaster relief. Many think it's synonymous with giving blood, but neither our government nor any other charity responds to emergencies from fire, hurricanes, floods, and other natural disasters to ensure the affected communities have safe shelter, food and fresh water.

Red Cross Afghanistan responded to the war by supporting hospitals, the disabled, sanitation, and prisons and communications. There's a lot of money in prison reform in the US, with prisons run by for-profit companies. The US has more people in prison than Russia or China...combined. Ponder that. There are two publicly traded prison companies on the stock exchange, and they represent roughly seventy percent of the total prison sector. Big money, and on all accounts, it appears they were branching out internationally.

Jake and Steve hit the jackpot, here. Our seven missing were busy working away, unbeknownst to anyone there. With so many volunteers in large charity organizations, it would be easy to conceal their true efforts, but the extra personnel there to guard them should have been a tip-off. Unlike in *Ad Astra*, where the missing scientist is trying to determine if there is additional life, these seven geniuses were procuring their own version of global eradication. What kind of sick people create something like this in the name of science? Makes you wonder if they were genetically modified, themselves. They would be, by the end...

Jake and Steve expertly and stealthily took care of the small security detail one by one. One of the scientists took notice and determined to take matters in his own hands, threatening, in some unknown dialect, to drop a vial which would take them all out. He might not have been speaking English, but when you scream erratically while holding something up and pointing to ground, you get the point. Here's the thing on bluffing: you need to be prepared to follow through. If not, then, consider yourself FUGAZI.

Jake walked over, with nerves of steel, to the instigator and promptly relieved him of his contents. He then grabbed his hand and insinuated that he would pour the vial on it. None of the other scientists protested vehemently, so he poured away. Guess it wasn't explosive or lethal, after all. The blow the scientist took to the head for threatening it was a whopper, though. He wouldn't make that false gesture again.

The scientists judiciously complied. The boys secured the rest of them after that, with only a few minor scrapes to the scientists. The scrapes were the result of taking trackers out of their forearms and inserting them into the security detail.

They 'deposited' the scientist's security team with their new trackers in a remote, secured location in the facility, but it would only buy us roughly twenty-four to thirty-six hours before they were found. Hopefully there was enough ventilation to sustain them, but we weren't really preoccupied with doing an exact calculation.

The clock was ticking.

I always loved that song *Time in a Bottle* by Jim Croce... *"But there never seems to be enough time, To do the things you want to do, Once you find them..."*

SEVENTEEN

Return

JAKE AND STEVE HAD SECURED the scientists for our flight home. The scientists wouldn't be traveling in their accustomed style. More like that ape in *Trading Places*. We didn't have time to debrief and interrogate them, and needed multiple language interpreters. Damn, we really needed to develop a new service for this. It would be a gold mine. I had Tom researching to purchase Pockettalk, a Japanese company that was on the cusp of launching a new language device that would change how we operate, especially in the military, education, and travel industries.

Traveling to Moscow, Beijing, Kabul, and now back State-side took us five days. Five hours to Moscow, seven to Beijing, sixteen to Kabul, and another eighteen hours to return to Dallas. Now add in the activities we had to perform in each location. This wasn't a job for the weak of heart.

We conferenced with Freddy, Bethany, and Tom on the flight home to discuss next steps with Williams. By time of our arrival back to the States, we could no longer hide under possible anonymity with the passing of Rogers, Azrail, Fu, and now, seven missing scientists. It would be all-out war.

Williams produced the President's Daily Briefing (PDB). You've seen the movie versions with *West Wing*, *House of Cards*,

VEEP, Designated Survivor, and the likes. The system is designed so the Director has no authority to give instructions or issue orders, but they do possess all the information collected from each of the agencies. Knowledge is the ultimate power.

We would force Williams to bring the fight to us. As everyone knows, everything is bigger in Texas. It was time to return to my perfect little hideaway home and the location of Fareed's capture. Upon my arrival at DFW Airport, I had a very special delivery, including two very special guests...Koda and Bruiser, my dogs. The best part of the day. We were together once again, and I'm not sure who was happier to see the other.

After my FUBAR incident, I went to a small town roughly ninety minutes east of Dallas to recuperate and recover. I hid from everyone and was away from my family for a total of twelve months during this process. Six months in a hospital in Landstuhl, Germany, where the doctors rebuilt me, and another six months in this small East Texas town, which allowed me to identify and plan the elimination of my enemies.

FUBAR – where sick psychos interrogated me for the location of vials I had hidden, beating the shit out of me to procure them. My head, liver, and spleen were lacerated. I had a hundred stitches in my head. All my ribs on my left side were broken, my lung collapsed, both rotator cuffs were torn, I sported road rash on whole left side from where I was dragged, I had a broken femur, broken wrist, my chin was obliterated, and I was missing teeth. The sick fucks had me tied to a chair while they took turns with the interrogation. My motto became, 'Let God have mercy on you, that's not my job.'

In this small town, I learned about the CIA's involvement and realized they were the tip of the iceberg, so to speak. Fareed, who had been a double agent for the CIA, stayed patiently with me during my extensive hospital recovery, waiting for me to slip up on the location of the vials that I possessed. It was here where I learned that Fareed was a twin and that his brother Abdul was also working for this absurd cause. They had me doing a rope-a-dope looking for a figment of their imagination. Actually, it was pretty brilliant on their part, considering.

My commander, Freddy, was also my next-door neighbor, unbeknownst to me. I had never seen him, and it was another year before I found out that he was my father. How messed up is that? Think I have trust issues? You betcha. He wanted to be near me to protect and look after me during my recovery.

This house was an architectural dream on a five-acre lot with easy access to the street and a manmade lake behind it. I had a long driveway entrance, as my house was nestled more towards the middle of the property line, with an infinity pool and a pond behind me before you hit the dock for the lake. It had beautiful stonework that covered the outside, with gas lanterns all around. It was U-shaped, with the front portion of the house a big great room with the kitchen, dining, and family room all together, with large open windows that looked out to the back's incredible views. Every side of the house opened to the center. Outside, in the center of the U, was the sparkling blue infinity pool with cascading falls, a diving board, and a swim-up bar. Trees were scattered all over the manicured lawn. The pond was about half an acre away, with a dog run on one side where I trained Bruiser and Koda.

The inside was even more grand. I installed state-of-the art surveillance and could tie into any server. I wasn't using the cheap shit the military secured by the lowest bidder. The best part was the arsenal that I had stored and mounted throughout the property. The two Stealth Recon Scouts came in real handy when we took out Fareed's posse of thirty.

I still remember Fareed telling me, "Those who don't fear death never die." Although he and his brother did eventually die, he was correct in this statement. There are so many tangled intricacies, it was an ever-evolving target that was nowhere near dying. I realized that I, myself, was becoming this motto.

What we could confirm was we had multiple countries and multiple internal and external agencies involved. We had artificial intelligence being used to mislead and misdirect on so many platforms, we lost count. Talk about creating paranoia. We had so many contributing factors, there was no way for it to be accidental or coincidental. We still hadn't come close to understanding what the final objectives and targets were. The ultimate success of a conspiracy is one that is unprovable—otherwise, they'd made a mistake. They seemed to always be one step ahead.

Here's what we did know. We had at least seven internal agencies compromised, along with China, Russia, and Afghanistan. We had seven scientists that we needed to confirm if they were working on a CRISPR/DNA coding modification. The scientists had recently secretly visited Antarctica, and we believed they were attempting to create their own versions of *Captain America*. Of course, reduce the population of the world by a billion, and you just changed the climate by 15%. Remember when Michael Douglas was asking for a 20% emissions policy in *American President*? Bingo. This is one way to do it quickly, verses over twenty years.

We originally believed 'they' (all parties involved) were attempting to distribute through upscale wineries to target/eliminate upscale political parties, but understood that, with technology, an airborne solution could easily be in play. *Thanks, technology.*

The number seven was repeating itself, and I don't believe in coincidences. So, who else was involved?

What is also associated with seven? The seven sins; pride, lust, envy, gluttony, wrath, sloth and the good ol' classic, greed. Dang, I would have pulled the trigger just like Brad Pit did in the movie *Seven*.

Time was running out.

EIGHTEEN

Groom Lake

WHEN I WAS DROPPED OFF IN TEXAS, the boys continued on to drop off our seven mysterious scientists.

Where do you take seven scientists to ensure their safety and preservation? Area 51, baby.

Area 51, located in Nevada, is a highly classified USAF facility that was acquired in the mid-1950s. Details of what is inside is not publicly known and lends to the conspiracy theories of UFOs and other myths. It was originally purchased for testing experimental aircraft and weapons systems. The surrounding lake, Groom Lake, is off limits to military and civilian air traffic, further leading to speculation about the base. The CIA has only finally acknowledged the base in the last five years after a freedom of information request was filed against the facility. Realistically, they probably finally did it after fifty years of dealing with crazy alien conspiracy whack-jobs.

The area around the base is a desert and is easy to miss if it wasn't for the warning signs: 'RESTRICTED AREA. NO TRESSPASING BEYOND THIS POINT. MILITARY INSTALLATION,' essentially screaming to come visit if you are a conspiracy nut. You have fields, cows, and mountains. It's one of those places where you feel like you are being watched and if you were not careful, you could disappear and never be found.

You have to wonder if art is imitating reality. In movies like *Independence Day* and *Men in Black* (both with Will Smith), you have the conspiracies of alien spacecraft, the undertakings of extraterrestrials, time travel, and teleportation, and don't forget, also, the Majestic 12.

Majestic 12 (MJ-12) is abundant in conspiracy theories. It was created under executive order by President Harry S. Truman and consists of an unproven secret committee of military, scientist, and government officials. The FBI declared its foundation to be bogus and a hoax, but activities associated with one world government are what caught our attention, due to the natural tie-in with our own recent events.

The FBI is currently the only agency within the six program managers under National Intelligence (Williams) where we do not presently have any confirmation of participation in the convoluted conspiracy that we were trying to dispel. Key word; currently.

The exact origin of each scientist's country was necessary to determine how wide of a net we needed to expand on our search. We had two from Russia, two from China, one for Afghanistan, one from US, and one other that Jake and Steve were working on confirming. I'm not sure how these scientists successfully communicated with each other, with multiple languages, but science is math, and it appears they were fluent in point and click.

The scientists would be parked here and would be well protected while we proceeded with the next steps. They would be under scrutiny from some of the same agencies we were monitoring. We had enlisted Ainsworth's services to admit the scientists and lord over them until we could determine the next steps. He was eager to comply as his final act before he took off for retirement to most assuredly chainsmoke his problems away and drink Coors in sandy bars with his beloved chow dog, Scully (which looked a little too uncannily like him).

NINETEEN

Prep for War

RETURNING TO TEXAS would either prove to be a superb move, or a failure. Failure wasn't an option. Williams would have clearance to see what had transpired here before and would be skeptical of us returning to the same location. By this time, she would also have confirmed that it wasn't just me, but that none of us perished in the explosions. She'd be reluctant to make the same mistake twice by allowing any of us to live, so we were betting she'd take off the safety measures for her next steps.

For our first hurdle, which would dictate everything else, we had to incentivize her to come to Texas. She would have every available personnel at her disposal looking for the gang, including my parents and children. We felt confident that she would not locate the others, so Freddy requested to be the bait, since he was already in Maryland and had the connections and incentive to get her here.

Jake and Steve were now on permanent kid patrol in NY. Although I would have preferred for them to be here for the showdown, the kids' long-term safety was my bigger priority. Tia was still in South America with my parents. Bes and Lily were on a recon and recover mission, with Aldo's help. Tom and Bethany were en route to meet me to help prep. Tom and I discussed (well, more like argued) his presence here, but in reality, we needed every physical body we could get, if this was to be successful.

The last time we were here, it was a night mission and we were able to utilize light and darkness in the heavily treed terrain to misdirect our thirty targets. Ultimately, we had Fareed enter the residence, where he was eventually maimed and captured. We were always on the offensive and led our opponents exactly where we wanted them. We would do so again. Hell hath no fury like a woman scorned. The paradox was that Williams and I both felt this way.

I watched on the monitors as Tom and Bethany drove down the long driveway entrance to the house and a smile crept onto my face. It had felt like months since I had seen him, and my heart ached for his embrace.

I opened the front doors and let the dogs out, who ran up to greet them. Tom walked confidently to the door and wrapped his arms around the small of my back, holding me cheek to cheek. "Nice to see you again Mrs. Baker," he said as he gently kissed my lips.

"Nice to see you, Mr. Baker," I whispered as I savored the embrace.

"Anyone going to help me unload here, or am I going to have to do it all by myself?" quipped Bethany.

"Your best friend has been in quite the mood lately," he whispered in my ear.

"I heard that. I'm right here. Mind you, I'm not deaf."

"We're coming, B," I stated exasperatedly as I winked at Tom, mouthing the letter B.

"Where do you want me to unload this? Want me to take it inside?" she continued.

"No, don't take inside. I'm thinking we are going *Braveheart* on this one."

"*Braveheart,* huh? Why do I get a sense that there's going to be a lot of manual labor in our immediate future?" Bethany feigned disapproval.

TWENTY

No Prisoners

AS TOM, BETHANY, AND I PREPPED, we waited for the charge and forthcoming phone call that Freddy prepared us for. Would it be hours, or days? Time would only tell.

The prep work was laborious, with the majority of it needing to be performed at night for fear that we were being monitored by satellite—and even then, the imaging could pick it up. We were certain that eyes were upon us, or would be.

The men that Williams would probably enlist would be private forces, most likely working for a subcontractor mercenary unit. She couldn't afford to bring in official special units on this. Military forces were acquainted with these merc organizations, albeit they were illegal under international law. Unlike private military contractors, these professionals would be hired with making money as their sole objective, with no regard to politics or interests. They understood the peril and inherit risks of the contract position, but ultimately, they wage war for those who pay the most, and also because they enjoy it. The question was: how many would she deploy? We hoped under twenty, but planned for up to a hundred.

Tom had the outdoor speakers playing while we worked. Judas Priest's *You Got Another Thing Coming* happened to be playing... "*If you think I'll sit around as the world goes by, you're thinking like a fool cause it's a case of do or die..."*

We all hummed while we continued to work, driven by the song selections, mentally visualizing and preparing for the showdown that was heading our way.

Once we had everything completed to our satisfaction, we went inside and again went over the game plan and possibilities, double and triple checking our work to ensure there were no errors. We ate, showered, and opened up a bottle of 1996 Masseto that Aldo had gifted me for the plane ride home.

"Here's to the end and new beginnings," Tom toasted as we clinked our glasses.

"It won't be the end. I'm not sure it ever will, but it *will* be the end of this festering pandemic that threatens not only us, but our nation and all that we serve to protect."

"I think I like what Tom said better. How about…here's to cutting off the head of a snake. Just die, already," added Bethany.

"Did you just quote from Knight and Day?" I smirked.

"That scene was so funny, it just makes me laugh. I've been waiting to use it."

"You two seriously have issues." Tom said as he shrugged his shoulders in amazement.

"You married her, so I'd put you in that category, too."

"Touché."

We sipped on the wine slowly and just sat quietly before Bethany astutely excused herself to give us a private moment.

"Promise me, love, that you'll retreat and go to the safe house if anything happens. Our kids…they can't lose both parents," I said with solemn conviction.

"As you've always said: if you prepared correctly, it shouldn't come to that," he responded.

"I've also said you can't reason with crazy, so…"

"When this is done, I want to be on a deserted beach and not in hiding, just lying there taking it all in for a very long time."

"What would we do?" I teased.

"Oh, I'm going to show you!" He said as he reached over to headlock me with a nuggie to my upper chest. I squealed and was still laughing when I overheard Bethany yell, "You realize I'm just in the next room, right?"

"I love you, babe. Today and always. You and me. Let's do this," I said as I brushed his hair back from his face and kissed his lips.

"Umm…it's me, too! You, him…and me. Let's not forget who took care of YOUR family when you were gone for 12 months!" Bethany yelled again from the other room.

***

It was 6:00 PM on day two when I finally received the call we had been waiting for from Jake.

"It's a GO. ETA under four hours. Package is confirmed. Four teams confirmed. Coming by land and water. You'll have two friendlies."

"Thanks, Jake. Be ready in case we need to go to Plan B."

"What's that?"

"Blow everything. I've sent you detailed instructions on how to do it remotely."

"I thought you were going to say that. Let's stick to Plan A, little firecracker. See you on the flip side."

"Roger that."

I turned to the Koda and Bruiser and instructed them to 'place', and they left immediately. I loved these dogs.

The next hours would be like a stakeout, waiting and watching. It was monotonous work, but one missed step could be fatal.

The three of us were in night gear, covered from head to toe. We hoped not to be detected through thermal imaging or infrared cameras, but also had to limit our movements so not to be detected through convection or conduction heat sources. More like in the movie *Predator,* having to meld into the hill...ever so silently waiting to make our move.

Tick. Tock. We heard the helicopter long before we could see anything, and anticipated they would drop off two teams by water, then circle around to drop two more teams by land.

It was another reason why I loved this house. The adjacent property was three times the size of mine, with a heliport on the west side. This allowed us additional time to prepare, as at least one team would have to travel further to get the normal flanking maneuver. One team would stay to protect Williams.

The best way to defend against a flanking team is to bend the line. Williams was opting for a total envelopment—basically, simultaneous attacks from three sides of us; back, side, and front. The far east side was littered with trees and overgrowth and would have been hard to defend or allow for a potential ambush on our part. She was short sighted (or grotesquely overconfident) in bringing only four teams.

Inside the house, we had it set up like *Home Alone,* with visual projections of Tom and me moving throughout the house with heat detectors. The audio recordings we performed earlier mirrored our planned moves. We even had the dogs throw in a bark or two to make it sound more realistic. This would allow for only a momentary reprieve, as we hoped they would think their equipment was not sighted correctly, but that small window was all we needed.

The sensors which we placed in the trees would trigger our next moves.

And so, we waited.

They would be proceeding at a careful rate, ensuring they were not making sounds, as well. Noise carried on this dark and cloudless night, which illuminated the grounds more than either party cared for.

Our limbs were starting to strain, as we had been holed up in the same position, now, for hours. It was closer to five hours before we had confirmed activity on their part, but we could sense their presence.

Our ears were perked. They were enveloping us and closing in. You could physically feel the closure. It was time to start.

3.2.1…

The visual projections were turned on in the house. Movement could be felt coming closer and then stopped, though no sound was made. We needed just a few more steps. *Come on, dammit.*

Another two minutes passed, and nothing triggered, still. It was a game of cat and mouse. Had the equipment malfunctioned?

Another minute. Nothing. Then came the glorious moment we had waited for. They had hit the mark, and Pavarotti's *Nessun Dorma* came blaring at a deafening level over the speakers that were installed throughout the property lines… *"il silenzio che ti fa mia…"* which translates to 'the silence that makes you mine.'

No lights turned on this time, as we didn't want them to see what was in store. We could tell that one party came in from the dock side, one coming in from a side angle and one coming from the front. Music off.

You have three options when you realize you've just been outed: freeze, flee, or fight. These were trained mercs, so yeah, they really only had one option.

The first group of four coming from the back side started moving more quickly, but in a controlled manner, with equal distance among them. They had another fifty feet to travel before they would reach our next checkpoint. Groups #2 and #3 were progressing as well, but were taking leads from group #1.

They had the same gear on as us, but now, with their increased movement and motions, we could detect them as we continued to not move and were one with the land.

Almost there…Europe's *The Final Countdown* came on just as the first group of four fell into a covered nine-foot ditch that we'd previously dug the day before. We actually dug over ten of these ditches, in preparation. As they would try to quickly maneuver to hoist each other up, Bethany used her crossbow to target the tanks we had set, along with the gasoline that was covering the floor length. The end result? A vapor that fills burnable mixtures with air, giving off heat and clouds, with black toxic smoke providing a flashback effect while being contained within the dugout. This was their gravesite, now. *Hasta la vista.*

The programmed Recons started firing.

Group #2 and #3 proceeded at full spring, now, as they witnessed the fire from the back side and the screams of their comrades, hoping to evade any bullets being sprayed across the terrain.

I should have left for my next position, but I paused to see the end result. As they got closer to the house entrances, they were firing M170 .50-calibur sniper rifles before they busted in. It was like the brother scene at the end of *The Accountant*. They were breaking without considering why they were allowed in. The two mercs we procured proved to be worth every extra penny we spent as they misdirected and allowed the remainder of their teams to enter the residence first, before shutting and securing the doors on them. They were now were using their own .50-caliburs to exit what they'd just entered, but it was too late. Tom allowed enough time for the two mercs to get to a safe distance before he pressed the detonator. The house imploded. The fire and smoke would be seen from miles, alerting our neighbors. *Damn, I really loved that house. We had thirty minutes max.*

I'd have to make up the extra thirty seconds I stayed, and jumped into the tunnel that made way to the adjacent property. Freddy had it formerly installed when I resided here as a way to check up on me, and added the security precaution in case an escape path was needed.

While Tom, Bethany, and our two new friends went to locate and take out team #4, who was guarding the perimeter of the adjacent property, I had free range underground, and got myself to the opening with the best 400-yard sprint I'd made in years. *That's right, I got it going on.*

Ironically, the secret underground entrance took me to the security room of the adjacent property. While a team member alerted everyone else about what they saw on the monitors, I would be undetected. I came to the top and listened and then did what any normal person would do...I whistled.

Bruiser, who was inside the room undetected, leapt and took care of this chap. The dog had his jowls over the merc's jugular. Blood spewed out in all directions, leaving him most surely incredulous as to how this had happened. How the hell did he not notice a dog in the room? Sloppy work. I just loved that dog.

When all was cleared, I entered the floor door and patted Bruiser's ears. "That's my good boy. Good job, buddy." I looked at the monitors and saw where the remaining team was, outside, and also noted the positions of our team. We had four on the ground to their remaining three. I felt anxious, but confident. I viewed the interior monitors for the room I needed to proceed to next. Freddy was bound, sitting on a chair.

Over the intercom, I heard, "Come and join us, Matti."

Show time.

TWENTY-ONE

Enlightenment

BRUISER AND I MADE OUR WAY to the library room of the house. I had him stop before we entered and motioned for him to stay back and remain alert by the front entrance.

The library was one of the first rooms behind the front foyer petition and was massive, with two stories of books adorning every inch of each wall. A winding staircase on one wall allowed you to go to the upper floor, with movable ladders still needed on each side so you could locate and pick your favorite selections. Books were organized like a library so you could find them by category: non-fiction, historical, fiction, children's, self-help, religious... First editions from Hemingway, Shakespeare, Jane Austen, and the like adorned the room with thriller/suspense authors Brad Thor, Stuart Woods, Lee Child, and Vince Flynn.

The executive desk towards the back of the room was massive, with intricate details on all sides. A colossal brown leather chair was behind it. There were at least three separate sitting areas with either a couch or side chairs around tables. There was a huge fireplace towards the back of the room that was unlit. Truly, it was an incredible, awe-inspiring room.

Williams was sitting in the colossal chair behind the desk, with Freddy sitting in a side chair ten feet away, his hands and feet bound by a zip tie.

"I'll have to give it to you, Matti, you've been difficult to procure. Please sit down and join us. I am curious, how did you manage to take out my teams?"

I looked to Freddy to get any type of read. He looked only momentarily at me and kept his stare focused on the wall. He'd been severely beaten and interrogated over the last forty-eight hours. I'm confident the only reason they kept him alive was just in case we ended up here.

I stayed standing. "It wasn't difficult. Of all people, you should understand…you know…when you are committed to a purpose."

"Ah yes, I'm afraid you are correct. We both share that quality."

We continued to stare at each other like a game of poker, waiting for someone to tip or give up their hand.

"We have been intertwined now for a long time, you and me. Did you know that?"

"I believe I met you for the first time after 9/11, at a congressional hearing," I offered.

"Oh no, we've been associates long before that." She looked over to Freddy and then said, "Freddy, have you not enlightened her after all this time? Such a shame."

I sat motionless, observing everything about her. Her wire rim glasses sat on the bridge of her nose. She was close to Freddy's age, dressed in a conservative pant suit with jacket, with what looked like a bulky bulletproof vest under it. She had her right hand concealed under the desk, while her left hand held a .475 Wildey Survivor Magnum, with its unique wood grip. Interesting choice, as it was one of the first gas-operated semi-auto pistols to reduce recoil for a more accurate and very quick shot.

"Nothing you want to ask, dear?" she stated sarcastically.

"Frankly, my dear, I don't give a damn."

"I heard you had quite the humorous side. Let's try this," she said as she pointed the gun towards Freddy.

Not only was Freddy beaten physically, but he looked broken, mentally. He looked at me with a sorrowful look. I'm not sure who he wanted me to kill, right then; her or him.

I had two options. I stalled. "If you feel a need to share, by all means, go for it—but please, start with the genesis."

"How fluent are you with our US presidential history?" she asked.

"Ever since I've been born and taken an oath to protect them and our nation, I'd say I'm better than average."

"Do you recall when Nixon received a set of panda bears?"

WTF? I was calculating the significance of this question as I responded, "Yes, I believe it caused quite the commotion at the time. Pandas were on the verge of extinction, and the United Sates was given a pair as a diplomatic rapprochement between us and China under Nixon's administration."

"Very astute of you. Do know what else was special about them?"

"I have the feeling you are going to enlighten me."

"Pandas eat for sixteen hours a day just to provide enough energy for their limited movements. Did you know they nurse their young for up to three years because of this?" she continued while I sat unmoving. "Well, let's get to the most important thing that you want to hear. Did you know that, a large percentage of the time pandas' birth in twins?"

My eyes dilated ever so slightly. My stomach tensed as I instinctively felt I was about to get hit with the blinding flash of the obvious that had alluded me all these years. I looked to Freddy, who kept his stare forward. Fareed, Rogers, Bale, Azrail…this whole messed-up posse I took out were all twins. This was no coincidence.

"Ahh, I see you didn't know, but you still can't put all the pieces together, can you?" she continued with a knowing smile.

"You see, the momma panda doesn't have enough energy to keep both of them alive, so she must choose which one to live, based on her instincts. It's simply survival of the fittest. Panda research not only will save other species, but it will save ours."

She's f'in cray-cray.

Based on how she emphasized 'survival of fittest' and the fact she was holding the gun in her left hand, it was all starting to become clearer to me.

Throughout evolution, only ten percent of the world's population is left-handed. Living in a right-dominate society, lefties learn to adapt and become stronger, and it is argued that they are more likely to think out of the box. Some argue that they even have decreased risks for health concerns. Oprah, Leonardo da Vinci, Barrack Obama, and Babe Ruth are all left-handed. You'll notice more singers, actors, and even presidents are left-handed, as they are deemed to be more creative than logical, as they've had to adapt to challenges. By all accounts, this last statement was certainly accurate, throwing logic right out the door.

"I guess we can throw out the Occam's Razor Theory here."

"You mean, all things being equal, the simplest explanation tends to be the right one? Oh, Matti, you do have a good sense of humor."

"So, you are trying to trick natural selection and create a new evolution? Is that what your secret society and the scientists are working on, attempting to recreate the lethal vials I have?"

Williams looked at Freddy dubiously. She vacillated from

disgust to incredulous in a matter of seconds. She stood up from the chair and pushed it back, allowing me to see her right hand, which concealing something.

"Don't try anything," she said as she showed me the detonator in her right hand while she held her gun in her left and pulled down the zipper on her vest to reveal C-4 strapped to her chest. *Oh shit, she cray-cray, alright.*

"By all accounts, it appears that Freddy may have misled you on something. Freddy, would you care to elaborate?"

Freddy closed his bloodshot eyes, a single tear rolling down his cheek. *What have you done?* My mind was flashing through every conversation, moment, mission; looking for the clues that were right in front of me this whole time. What have I missed?!

"Lethal is a correct term, but by your reaction, I'd say you have no idea what you possessed this whole time, and why so many people are looking for it and you. Science will obliterate religion, with what we will accomplish." She was in front of the desk, now, leaning on it.

"What has your Fred, here, told you about your birth?" she continued now, in a heightened knowing stance.

"Stop." It was the first time Freddy had spoken since I arrived, his head dangling over his chest, and it came out as a whisper.

"Oh, stop it, Freddy, we're just getting to the good part," she said excitedly. "You see, Matti, your mother was the tip of the experiment. You and your siblings were the true results." *Siblings? Did she just say siblings with an 's'?* I looked to Freddy as I heard gunshots outside. Our time was running out. I couldn't let the others come near while she had C-4 strapped to her chest. You can't reason with crazy.

"My siblings?" I asked, stone-faced, as I looked back to Freddy and Williams.

"You're a triplet. You were the exception to the experiment. Just like your children. What, did you think that was just a natural birth? Which agency do you think created those online DNA geometrics that buyers want use to prove their ancestry? It's brilliant that consumers are electively providing us the tools we need to accomplish our final goals. The DNA coding was right out of a Captain America comic book, but no one thought that you…a woman…would end up being the superior gene."

She quickly turned her body to Freddy with a look of disdain on her face. "You are no further use to me," she said, and shot him in the chest. His body slumped instantly into lifelessness in the chair.

Oh, God. Noooooo!

"We've wasted enough time. Tell me where the vials are, or your kids will lose their mother. You try anything and we both will meet our maker," she threatened as she held the detonator out in front of me with her thumb high above it.

I sat there, confused but enraged, and finally said, "You know what the difference is between a Wildey and a Bruno?"

Her eyes got wide, calculating. I just played the trump card, and with that, I calmly said "Koda" and immediately pulled the trigger.

TWENTY-TWO

Lights Out

KODA LEAPT FROM HIS STATUE POSITION in the library and had her right forearm in his mouth, tearing through to the bone. There were so many stuffed bears, ducks, and wildlife in the library room that it was never considered to be out of the norm for a treasured pet to be on display. There was no way she had any muscle control to have her thumb press anything, as he bit right through her arm, releasing the detonator to the ground. She wouldn't need to worry about using that hand anymore.

At the same time as Koda went for the right hand, I pulled out my 7.5 FK Bruno Field Pistol and shot her in her left shoulder, forcing her to drop her gun due to the impact. The Bruno has a double-stack mag, red grip, single action, tilting barrel with a proprietary recoil system. Its range is 2000 feet per second versus the Wildey at 1850 feet, so that would be the answer to my question, but both are generally regarded as some of the fastest pistols on the market.

I launched over a couch to pick up her gun, grabbed the detonator, and then ran to Freddy, who was not moving. I couldn't make out any vitals on him, either. It appeared she'd shot him just above the heart valve. Concerned that she had a Plan B or C in store, I whistled for Bruiser to enter and, together with Koda, we started to haul Freddy quickly out the front door as I pressed my hand to his chest to try to stop the bleeding.

I was leery of turning on my earpiece and talking or alerting the others, as I was unsure if they were in the clear from the last team that surrounded the house. I prayed the gunshots I'd heard outside were those of us taking out her last team, with no casualties on our part.

As we passed the library entrance, I commanded the dogs to keep going while I turned back to retrieve Williams. With her glasses thrown off, her hair in disarray, and the remains of her right hand on the floor, I saw her tapping on her chest with her limp left hand while blood continued to trickle down.

Time. It all boils down to time. How many digits in the code? How many had she already pressed? How far could I get?

There are only two things that we are inherently afraid of: falling, and loud noises. All other fears are learned. It was a matter of time. I had no time. I was attempting to run back towards the entrance when I saw Tom entering and yelled, "*Nooooo!*" with fear in my voice.

That was the last thing I said.

They say the last thing you see before you die is your children. I thought maybe I'd see a montage, like Bruce Willis did at the end of *Armageddon*.

I saw nothing.

TWENTY-THREE

Last Goodbye

Ten days later…

THERE WAS A SMALL but intimate gathering at St. Matthew's the Apostle Cathedral in Washington, D.C. Red brick and terra cotta trimmed the exterior, while the inside is opulently decorated in precious stones and marble, with a large mosaic of Matthew. This church has hosted its share of notable masses with JFK, Pope John Paul II, and famous senators.

Security was tight, with roads blocked and armored cars and snipers on rooftops. This was not your typical funeral. There were red reserve banners over the first three rows of pews. White flowers and photos on easels adorned both sides of the pulpit.

Matthew, Mary, and Mark were in a private room before the ceremony started.

"I still can't believe we are here, it's surreal." Mary said somberly. She was wearing a black dress with a simple choker strand of her mother's pearls.

"I just…I just don't know where to begin. Everything already is so different. Did Grandma and Grampy make it in time? Are they seated already?" added Mark, who wore a black Armani suit.

"Please, you two. I need to concentrate right now. I can't mess this up," Matthew said, exasperated, pulling at the black tie that was choking him.

"Just breathe. Breathe in, breathe out. We have time. Why don't you practice one more time on us?" Mary offered.

"Yeah, that will help. Let me go over it from the beginning. Both of you sit over here, as I'll need to look to you for reassurances during it." Mary and Mark pulled up chairs and seated themselves, while Matthew settled himself behind a table.

"Good evening. I am Matthew Baker, Matti and Tom's son. On behalf of my sister, Mary, and brother Mark, we want to thank everyone who traveled here to pay their respects to our parents. Additionally, we have some dignitaries here that our family would personally like to thank for their assistance during this difficult time: The President and First Lady of the Unites States...thank you. Additionally, Archbishop DeVita, CIA Directors Long and Sedlin, and FBI Director Coles. Thank you for your support.

"We wanted to share with you first about our mother, Matti. For being the most outgoing person we knew, she was also very private and reserved, at times. If she was here, she would tell us to not dwell on the past and also would say that we shouldn't shed a tear for her now that she is gone. The three of us always strived to meet her wishes, but we're sorry, Mom. We won't be able to accommodate this last request.

"To honor her wishes, though, I won't go into laborious detail about her past. For those that knew her in her early years or her working years, we look forward to hearing your stories after the service – and please don't hold back. She wouldn't want you to. She wanted this to be a celebration of life.

"Just the basic info...Mom was born into a military Catholic family. She would joke that when she was younger, she preferred nerf guns and footballs over Barbie dolls and nail polish. She often said in her younger schooling years that she was a little wild, with her motto being 'you only live once.'

"Gregarious in nature, she felt that her life started when she met our father when she was working an assignment. She told us of their first date and how he kissed her gently on her forehead at the end of the evening, and she said she knew he was the one. In fairness, he did, too. From that day, Mom and Dad were best friends and partners in everything. She felt he made her life complete.

"With the three of us, she was always there helping; be it as homeroom mother, talent show chair, serving on PTO exec boards, on athletics and cheer boards, football ... you name it. We never thought much of it at the time, as we just thought that was what all moms do. As we're sure is the case with most parents' wishes, Mom wanted to make sure we had a better life than she, and strived to help us reach our full potential. In looking back, we're not sure how she managed it all, but she always did.

"If you didn't know, Mom loved high school sports, especially sports where she could yell. Now, if you never heard this petite woman, she had lungs that blasted for miles and could be heard in any stadium. Ask anyone for game footage and you most likely will hear her in the background on the audio: "Get down the field! That's holding!" Or, a classic to the refs..."You have one job!"

"Mom also loved action movies or anything from the eighties and nineties, and songs from the seventies. If left alone, you could guarantee that she had either a Mel Gibson, Bruce Willis, Tom Cruise, Keanu Reeves, or Kurt Russell movie on and could recite lines with the best of them.

"Mom was completely tone deaf and, honestly, a terrible dancer, but that didn't stop her from trying, despite our persistent pleas to stop. Tom Petty was her favorite musician, but she had an eccentric mix of artists on her playlist, with many songs mixed in from our elementary talent show performances.

"Mom enjoyed a good bottle of wine and loved to share a bottle... or more...with friends. Sorry, Archbishop. We know she is sharing a drink with her mother at the Pearly Gates, and catching up.

"Mom had a few close friends and family that she trusted. So as not to leave out any names, I'll just mention two with Bethany and Freddy, who had been with her the longest, and her other companions in life outside of our Dad. She valued and treasured your relationships.

"We've had many animals over the years, but there is no doubt that Mom was a dog person. She would walk with our dogs down the neighborhood path, listening to music or talking to friends, always with one earpiece in and one out – always on alert. We honestly don't know how our current dogs will handle her being gone, as she was their life. We know that she is with her former German shepherds and labs, now, taking them all for the best walk ever.

"Mom never shared much of her working years with us. We knew she had different positions and assignments, and she seemed to excel in all that she did. When pressed, she'd just say she did what she had to do, but from the people in attendance today, we'd say that she had a huge and everlasting impact. She felt patriotic in helping others, based on her many experiences, and possessed a deep loyalty to her country.

"Mom did share with us a few stories of her past that held much adversity, but she always prevailed. As children, we often dismissed her experiences and wisdom, but as we've now growing older, we understand that she is the true definition of a survivor. She would sometimes write, but her true gift was storytelling. Mom always said, 'Never let the truth get in the way of a good story.' We weren't sure, at times, what was fact or fiction. Honestly, I don't think she did, either. Family and friends referred to her as the ultimate Aesop Fable Teller.

"As siblings, we have always joked between ourselves about who Mom loved most, but honestly, she made sure that each of us was her favorite. We are blessed.

"Many have described our mother as a driven leader, determined, strong, vigilant, and passionate. We hope we possess just a few of these attributes as we carry her legacy forward.

"We thank you for coming today to bid your well wishes, and in the spirit of our mother, we hope you join us afterwards for a toast and merriment. Mom's final wishes were for us to throw her ashes off a pier, let the wind take her, and to say 'she's dead' and move forward, but we can assure you, she has never been more alive than inside each of us."

There was a long pause before Matthew spoke. "Do you think that works?"

"Oh, crap, we don't have time to practice Dad's," he added as he checked the time on his watch.

"There were one or two spots you said I versus us or we, but other than that, she would be happy," Mary offered.

"I'm glad you're doing this and not me. Let's get this over with," Mark said as he got out of his seat and sternly headed into the sanctuary.

TWENTY-FOUR

White Sands

ILHA GRANDE ISLAND OFF THE COAST of Rio de Janeiro in Brazil is now a popular tourist destination, but still has some areas that are largely undeveloped. Due to its remote location, it originally housed a leper colony and a top security prison. Average temperatures are in the low 80s. The island has a biological reserve in the southwestern point that incorporates roughly eighty-five hundred acres, with half of those covered in dense Atlantic Forest.

The contrasting forest of the reserve settles on the ocean mix of blue and translucent green, with white beaches and rock protrusions. It's an unspoiled location for relaxation if you do not want to be disturbed.

No motor vehicles are on the remote island, and only way to get to Ilha is by ferry or, if you happen to be in the remote reserves, by private boat.

Laying under a green umbrella, with a tropical drink in one hand and an up-and-coming indie author book in the other, I was being pinged on the tactical high-frequency satellite com. Lightweight and compact, with multiple levels of encryption and frequency hopping, there were only two people that could be using this to contact me. *Damn, I just wanted to finish this last chapter.*

"Yes, who's calling?" I asked.

"I just attended your funeral. It was nicely done, and your children did an excellent job."

I had a smile of pride on my face, hearing this, and tried to visualize what had transpired. I made a mental note to look at the video later.

"That's nice to hear," was all I responded.

"On behalf of myself and everyone, we are forever grateful and indebted for your services."

"Thank you. How's our patient doing?"

"He's a bit grouchy, but he's out of the woods now, and should be able to join you in a few weeks."

"And the other arrangements?"

"All of your requests are being addressed as we speak."

"That's nice to hear."

"Ms. Baker, you hit just the tip of the iceberg, so to speak. When you're ready, we would prefer to enlist your services."

"I'm sure you would. I'll contact you when I'm ready."

"By chance, any time frame on that?"

"Now, now, Mr. President…as I said…when I'm ready. Thank you for calling, and my best to the missus," I said, and promptly hung up.

I looked over at Tom and smiled. He was sound asleep to the ocean waves. Kenny Chesney was playing *When the Sun Goes Down* "*… Watchin' you sleep in the evenin' light, Restin' up for a long, long night…*"

His arm was still in a sling, and it was making quite the suntan mark, as he had the strap over his chest.

I looked out at the ocean with the gentle waves rolling and cloudless sky, and searched the horizon. I repositioned the lounger and flipped the page of my latest thriller book.

Tomorrow it would all be different, and I was content.

TWENTY-FIVE

Juntos

THE NEXT DAY, we did more of the same and set up our spots on the beach to take in the breathtaking views. More importantly, we waited for the evening arrival.

We had a feast of seafood paella and chilled bottles of Chevalier Montrachet D'Auvenay awaiting our guests. Tonight, we would celebrate.

Time has a way of slowing down when you are not connected to the world. What you don't know can't hurt you (the infamously mistaken phrase 'Ignorance is bliss', an 18th-century ode by Thomas Gray, forgets the second part of the phrase, 'tis folly to be wise.')

Tom encouraged me to relax and let it go for now, but that wasn't necessarily my nature. I took another sip of wine and continued to stare out at the water while thousands of thoughts flashed through my head.

My eyes were just about to close when I saw the shadow at the edge of the horizon slowly getting bigger. I got out the binoculars to verify.

Tom was snorkeling in the water and I yelled to him and pointed. Although I loved the sounds of ocean water, I wasn't necessarily fond of snorkeling with fish swimming all around me. Some find it exciting. I was not one of them.

It seemed to take forever for the vessel to approach, but eventually

I saw the passengers all lined up on the rail, waving excitedly. I counted. One, two, three, four, five, six, seven, eight, and nine, with four additional furry ones for good measure. They were all here.

The yacht stopped four hundred feet out and two dingys hauled the passengers toward the shoreline. The kids and dogs jumped out before it stopped, and we all embraced and fell, laughing, in the water while the dogs hammed it up, splashing. Scout and Trooper, the family labs that Tom and the kids acquired while I was away, acted like they were in heaven. Koda and Bruiser were already on alert.

My entire extended family was back together. I had a momentary uneasy feeling, as it was similar to the last time at the restaurant, sans kids and dogs.

Tom, Jake, and Steve helped my parents and Tia unload, while Bethany came over to hug me and punch me on the arm. "It can never be easy with you, can it? Good lord, woman, I don't have to worry about our enemies getting me—you're going to give me a heart attack, first."

"I missed you, too," I said as I continued to hold onto her. "Thanks for your help on the scene. It was a last-minute call and I needed it to feel and look real. You did great."

"Killing me, woman. The kids did a nice job, by the way. I'm guessing they may be a little messed up, having to write their parents' pretend eulogies, so take that into consideration. Auntie Bethany came through, as always. Damn, do you owe me big. Again, just saying. Let's get changed and comfy, then we can sit down, and you can give us the lowdown. I'm sure this is a tale of all tales."

"I owe you more than I can ever repay. What can I say? You're blessed to have me in your life." I gave my widest smile, showing all my teeth, and got another arm punch for that. Crap, she is f'in strong. That's going to leave a mark.

Jake and Steve did a perimeter search of the property and came back saying how it mirrored Tom Cruise's hideout in *Knight and Day*. How funny, it really did—and how ironic that Bethany had just quoted that movie. Hmm.

Our location was perfectly secluded, with a large house to accommodate all of us with full amenities, but we also had a full comm center, speed boat, helicopter, and enough ammo to blow anyone to kingdom come. I liked it here.

We gathered outside around a large teak dining table and ate and drank and made small talk. I thought about all the holidays that were missed because of various missions or assignments or scheduling conflicts, and wished it could be like this all the time.

I noticed Bethany was seated next to Steve…again. She wasn't getting out of here until she fessed up.

Mark used his fork to tap his water glass to get everyone's attention. "Mom, since we're all finally here, can you go into some details of what actually transpired? I mean, we just had to give your eulogy, so I think we deserve that, at least."

Matthew quickly added, "We? You have a mouse in your pocket? I think 'I' had to do all the heavy legwork."

"Wait, I helped write the majority of it!" added Mary.

"Ok, ok…stop…I give. Let me give you the condensed version for now, so we can all enjoy our evening under these beautiful stars."

I looked towards my aging parents, who I have purposely kept in the dark about most of my profession's activities. There are things a parent shouldn't know about their children, and this was a good example of one of them. I think they deserved more truth, after what I've put them through these last weeks.

"In a nutshell, we've been working to uncover some corrupt parties both internationally and, unfortunately, on US soil, as well. The survival instinct is humanity's single greatest inspiration, but with human nature, whatever your intentions, if you have the ability to do something, you will, sooner or later. Temptation can't be resisted forever. This is such a case.

"We have confirmation of several internal government agencies, along with Russia, China and the Middle East, in collusion to genetically mutate DNA in vain efforts to create a controlled species and have global impact on religious fronts. An enemy that controls or knows the future can't lose."

"How can you stop it?" asked Mark.

"Well, I can't do it alone. That's why I reached out to some friends over at the FBI when I noticed that trend of DNA manipulation. The FBI is the owner of a CODIS database and software. CODIS is the Combined DNA Index System which houses all criminal DNA and is used as a tool to aid federal, state, and local crime labs in comparing and matching DNA profiles. There're three levels of protocol and security measures in place. The highest level, NDIS (or National DNA Index System) is managed solely by the FBI. It was a risk, as the FBI was under Williams's umbrella, her being the Director of National Intelligence. Without the FBI's knowledge, she had been using this information with other countries and scientists to create their version of a New World Order."

"Since she had the highest security clearance and worked for the US for decades, what was her motivation?" asked my father.

"It appears she and others that she enlisted had a twin fascination, as part of a pre-determined natural selection, with dominating the world by creating a controlled species. With her death, who knows what her ultimate motivation was, but it could provide an opportunity to create the perfect weapon while using technology to destroy the church. With my mother's death, scientists had created what they thought would be the perfect weapons, only something didn't go as planned, and instead of twins, triplets came out. Did Freddy ever tell you that I had siblings?" I directed the question to my parents.

My mother gasped, processing the sheer gravity of what I was saying. "No! No, he never mentioned anything. Our only contact with him was limited. He wanted you to grow up as normally as possible, given the circumstances, and we had his number to contact him only in case of an emergency. We did contact him when you were young when we realized you were far more advanced than children your same age. That's when Tia came on board."

"So, you're like a super bot?" inquired Mark.

"Well, I'm not sure of that," I laughed, "but the US has invested a large sum of money on me, and has a vested interest in my actions. Apparently, they have not been able to recreate the sequencing and need either me or the vials I possess to bring them to fruition."

Tom looked at me with a concerned look, as the next question would be inevitable.

"Wait. If you possess it, then doesn't that mean that we do, too?" Mary asked anxiously as she looked at her brothers.

"Partially, but you wouldn't have the whole key, since your father was not part of the original trial. That's why it was imperative that it looked like Freddy and I died in the explosion. That eliminates some of their options."

"So, whichever person, agency, or country remains in this quest, their only options are to recreate it on their own or find the vials?" asked my father again.

"Since they have not been able to recreate it in decades, the more favorable option would be to locate the vials, which Aldo and my new friends are procuring as we speak so we can permanently remove...Or, another option for them…they need to locate my long-lost siblings, which by all accounts appears they have not been successful in locating or capturing."

"Oh, crap, I didn't even process that," added Bethany.

"Obviously, I'll need to visit Freddy when he gets out of ICU and obtain some crucial information for next steps."

"Bethany hasn't filled us in. How did you escape the explosion and fake your own death?" asked Jake.

"Ahh. Williams had C4 strapped around her chest and, versus using a hand detonator (due to the loss of her arm, thanks to Koda), she was manually entering the code into a backup terminal she had on her vest. Since she was shot in her shoulder, it restricted her from entering the code quickly, allowing Tom and I much needed extra seconds. The average blast radius is five feet, and is in a sphere. Casualties and injuries are as result of the other items that are projected at high velocity speeds, which are often fatal. I was just past the front entrance of those massive iron doors, which took the blunt of it. I was propelled onto your father, who broke my fall."

"That was no picnic. Just saying," Tom added.

"Based on the first explosion, fire and medical had already been dispatched, and they arrived shortly after the second explosion. As the medics were frantically working on Freddy, Bethany administered a long-term beta blocker to Tom and me at the scene to slow our heartrates down to a level that the untrained medics in East Texas took for death. Our two new merc pals helped assist with Freddy at the hospital with doing the same. It was then just a matter of paying and redirecting personnel at the hospital while we all were transferred to our final resting place."

"It's just crazy, listening to all of this. I don't know how you do it," Mom contributed.

"I agree it is crazy. It takes imagination in a war against reality."

"So, what is our next move?" inquired Bethany.

"For the time being, we're going to enjoy some sandy beaches and some much-needed R&R. After that, I need to talk to Freddy and see Aldo and lock down some loose ends, but hopefully we'll be able to start some new adventures. Jake and Steve can train the kids, and my parents can return to their normal life."

"What about you, Mom and Dad, since everyone thinks you are dead?"

"Ha. Haven't you ever seen the *Friday 13th* movies? He never dies. Napoleon once said, 'There are no bad regiments, only bad colonels', and I'm afraid we still need to determine who else is out there before we can resurface. In the meantime, we're going to do some research and will invest in data storage and language translation companies. It's going to be a goldmine. I recommend that everyone to do the same, too."

TWENTY-SIX

Papa

WE BASKED FOR WEEKS in South America, enjoying the natural surroundings and solitude. While Tom and I planned our days, with the kids and my parents exploring, at night we gathered with Bethany and the boys to strategize. We were now the Five Musketeers…All for one, one for all.

I had two trips that required my attention. One was to meet with Freddy and the other to obtain a very special package. Freddy needed to happen, first. Bethany, Tia, and I ferried over to Angra dos Reis, then Bethany flew us to the States, dropping off Tia first while we continued to make our way up north. While we were gone, the others made preparations for our return. Bethany reminded me again of how good of an investment this plane was.

Freddy had insinuated all my life that the vials were for global destruction. I incorrectly assumed they'd be instantly lethal, but the true impact on society was long-term.

I always wondered why he gave them to me, a child, to possess, but humans tend to take things for granted when it comes from family.

Freddy never surfaced in my life until I reached out to him to help me enter private contractor training against my parents' wishes. To me, he was the ever-covert 'Charlie' in *Charlie's Angels,* and became my commander, me never having seen him but knowing him as the voice in my earpiece and in life. He brought Bethany and me together and coordinated all of our missions and assignments. I had a yearning to meet him all the years, only to find out he was there the whole time. The betrayal I felt at finding out, I continue to deal with. Now, couple this with my discovery that I was not alone, but had two siblings that had been hidden from me. Betrayal was just one of the feelings I felt towards Freddy.

To top it off, I only recently discovered that he was my birth father. As I was tracking Tammy Carter, the former Deputy Director of the CIA who also was part of this screwed-up conspiracy, I discovered Freddy by mistake. That, in turn, ended in her ultimate demise and brought us full circle to the restaurant where we were targeted for elimination. Freddy was the constant in all of this, which lent to asking about his true motivations, as people had a habit of dying because of associating with him.

I traveled incognito to Walter Reed National Military Medical Center in Bethesda, Maryland. Walter Reed is one of the most prominent US military medical facilities, and has served numerous presidents. In fact, the secret service had the autopsy of JFK's performed there, versus the Dallas hospital. I'd always wondered why. Freddy was transported there from Tyler, Texas after he was stabilized and able to be moved.

I did not attempt to contact Freddy before this, as I needed time to reflect on the events that had transpired and the transgressions of my father, innocent or not.

He had just returned to his hospital room after physical therapy when I arrived in blue scrubs, sporting a messy bun. My name tag showed I was nurse Taylor Jenkins. I previously used this name when I met Scott Bartik, who was a House Representative and the

Chair of Agriculture. He also happened to be a twin, and met his demise on a super yacht. He was recruited by Carter and was into some kinky shit, by all accounts.

Freddy was reading something on his phone when I interrupted with, "Anything interesting?"

His momentary surprised look quickly dissipated and was replaced with earnest appreciation. "I was wondering how long it'd be before you made contact and was hoping to see you sooner than later."

"I've been a little busy playing dead for the world to see."

"I see you had a wonderful ceremony with some notable dignitaries," he stated.

"All for perception. The Archbishop owed me one for a favor I did in the past, and who knew that Sedlin and Long were actually good guys? And, quite frankly, the President and the FBI were just thankful that I did not blow this up in the media, which would have blown up in their faces. I hear your service was well-attended, as well."

"I'm so sorry, Matti."

Freddy had masterminded my whole existence. He abandoned me after my mother died, leaving me with my aunt and uncle. He manipulated the true intent of the vials he'd left with me. He participated in my training. He arranged for Bethany to be in the same training. He leveraged Tom's father's automation industry, making Tom a potential suitor. He sent me on countless missions where the true objective was misled. He was responsible for my twelve-month FUBAR and time missed with my family. He was the one that had us tracked to the restaurant, which almost led to our demise. He concealed his true identity from me for decades, and now I find out that I have two siblings. WTF.

He also secretly aided me on so many different levels that it left me conflicted as to his intentions. When I found out his true identity, I confronted him and memorized verbatim what he said to me..."*I'm sorry. I'm sorry I didn't trust enough in you, me, or this world, and that I let all this time go between us. I've watched you from afar for so long that I convinced myself it couldn't ever be any other way. I've been monitoring life, looking in from the outside for so many years, I don't know what is real anymore. So many times, I wanted to tell you the truth, but feared the lies had become your new reality. How would you ever believe anything? It was a no-win situation any way I played it.*"

"You've told me you were sorry, before. You know what the definition of insanity is? Doing the same thing over and over and expecting a different result," I said solemnly.

"Matti, there've been so many moving parts and parties, it's impossible to fathom or understand it all. I tried the best that I could with the information I had at the time. As a parent yourself, hopefully you understand that."

"Who and where are they?" I asked while I stared unwaveringly into his eyes.

"Your siblings?"

"Who else would I be inquiring about? Don't stall, Freddy. It's unbecoming, and you've misled me long enough, don't you agree?"

"All I was privy to at the time was that you have two brothers. One went to a top-secret program under the CIA and the other went to Russia. Their mission was to turn them into super assassins. From what I follow, they appeared to be very successful at meeting that objective, but our paths have never crossed."

"And my mission? Have you manipulated it all this time to ensure that I was the best of the best?"

"No. I wanted you to be far away from it, but knew that inevitably it was in your DNA. Trauma, strength, love, abandonment—whatever the characteristics are, they were transferred into your DNA. You were created to be the host for generations to come—the ultimate military weapon."

"All these years you lied to me in regard to the purpose of the vials…leading me to believe I was the sole possessor of the world's judgment. You had me go on rat chases and rope-a-dope missions, all as part of a smokescreen. Why?"

"It was the only way I could ensure your safety. I was trying to protect you. I lost your mother; I couldn't lose you too."

"As I stand here in front of you, you still continue to lie to me."

"Matti, I'm telling you all that I know, now."

"Freddy, you're failing to mention THE big point, don't you think?"

"What is that?" he asked sincerely.

"You are not my father."

His eyes teared, but nothing ran down his face. He sat on his bed, broken and defeated. "No, but I wanted to be and honestly felt that I was. You are all that I have left…How did you know?"

"They would have been targeting you, if you were the original host provider. The fact that they were not, indicates that you are not."

"It was a blind trial with multiple specimens, but I wanted it to be me. I hoped and wished it was me. The others did it for money, I was involved because I was in love with your mother."

"That's how you got Williams to come to Texas isn't it? She had to believe that you were part of the original experiment, as you were privy to details only a few select would know. She needed you alive in case she couldn't procure me or the vials."

"I've always intimated I was your father and let her and others believe that all these years."

The definition of a father is a man in relation to his child and the importance and role we place on them in society. My uncle raised me, and I considered him my father. This man in front of me, with no biological connection—was he not also a father figure, protecting and guiding me while making mistakes along the way?

I was in the same scenario as Tom Sizemore in *Sins of the Father,* having to decide whether to protect this man or let justice be served.

I already sensed the answer to the question that I had to ask and know the answer to... "Who and where are the other potential suitors?"

"They died with your mother," he shakily responded, and stopped momentarily before proceeding. "Immediately after your birth, all of them were massacred in the delivery room with sarin nerve gas. Since I was not part of the program, I wasn't in the room at the time. I went to the NICU and was only able to take one. I took you, per your mother's request."

"Why would she agree to be part of this test?"

"They convinced her it was her patriotic duty to save the world and that only she was qualified to do it. You have to remember that it was a decade full of unrest, with the conclusion of Vietnam War, the oil crisis, the Arab-Israeli conflict, and the Afghan War. Apollo 13 had aborted, and the nuclear age was not just present, but looming. Just as the Manhattan Project was created to produce the first nuclear weapons, the NWO Project was created in the event that there was another world war."

I sat there momentarily motionless, trying to process all the particulars and ramifications, my head spinning on hearing 'NWO.'

New World Order.

"Why have only I been targeted and not my siblings?"

"This experiment was back in the '70s. It was a male-only dominated field. Their intent was to genetically alter twin boys for the world's survival. You alone hold the gene sequencing that dominates over all others, what they now consider the ultimate weapon."

"Why didn't the same scientists simply recreate it after our birth?"

Freddy looked at me in total despair in the moment that he'd never wanted to come to fruition; that he lived over and over in his head. "Matti, your mother had almost nine months to reflect and understand the long-term consequences of her actions. It was she who administered the gas to kill them all. It was the only way to ensure it wouldn't happen again, by taking them all out together."

My heart sank.

TWENTY-SEVEN

Extraction

WE STILL HAD PLAYERS-at-large in this game. Afghanistan was not the only player left that had not been contained or detained. The other scientist was confirmed to be Palestinian. F'me. Could we add any more to this? Israel is the only Jewish state, while Palestine is Arab. The Israeli-Palestinian conflict boils down to who gets what land and who governs it. Trust me, there is nothing simple about any of this. Let's not forget: it was Israel who created Pegasus spyware, enabling their law enforcement remote surveillance of smartphones. If only it had stopped at law enforcement.

Guess where the vials are? Yep. Palestine's enemies. Add the recent recognition by the US of Jerusalem as the new capital of Israel, and the timing couldn't be worse.

Bessum and Lily traveled to Jerusalem under the disguise of sister/brother with a local church mission group. The visual of Lily with Azrail still sat uncomfortably in my head. The news reported that Azrail had a heart attack in a hotel. There was no mention of the tie marks on his hands and feet, or the fact the heart attack was brought about by suffocation.

Overlooking the walls of Old Jerusalem, on a hill in Mount Olive, sits the Garden of Gethsemane. It was here that Roman soldiers arrested Jesus before his crucifixion. Having been raised

Catholic, I recalled their teachings of its importance, as it demonstrated Christ had shared in the human condition. St. Paul said, "He became poor, so that through his poverty you might be rich."

I'd selected this area to store the vials due to the massive olive trees that adorn the area, and if it did create world destruction, as I believed at the time, it should be where HIS life was taken. It was noted that he prayed thrice, checking on the three apostles between each prayer and finding them asleep. *"The spirit is willing, but the flesh is weak."*

The number three consumed me now, with news of my brothers and my own children, a trilogy in our own making.

I had provided a map to Bessum and Lily, as the vials were encased in the root of one of the massive trees and they would need to carefully dig it out with the assistance of a metal detector. Once they made it to the grounds, they changed into ground service uniforms so they could perform their task without drawing additional attention. I felt confident that Lily would not be pleased or accustomed to this outfit. Paybacks were going to be a bitch on this one, but were necessary.

As the trees and grounds had grown substantially over the years, they initially had some trouble identifying the exact location. Admission is free to the garden, so the barrage of mission groups and visitors was sporadic, further delaying their efforts, but they prevailed.

The vials were encased in the smallest custom fireproof, waterproof, weather-resistant, dual-locking container. It was tamper-proof and destruction-proof. I'd chosen the same safe maker that I'd used before, to bring Fareed to his ultimate capture. I'm a big fan of loyalty rewards.

Upon procuring it, Bessum and Lily promptly left the site to rendezvous with Aldo in Tel Aviv. They were all now part of my extended family, and I trusted them. They dropped the vials to Aldo and he in turn headed to the US to drop off the precious cargo.

When I left Ihla, I brought Tia along with me, but dropped her off first to meet Aldo. My explanation was she was to obtain the vials for me while I was visiting Freddy, in hopes that another connection might be made in the interim. It couldn't hurt to try— just saying.

TWENTY-EIGHT

Outer Space

THERE HAVE BEEN OVER 135 space shuttle missions carried out by NASA since 1969. *Damn, another organization that ends in 'a'.*

These missions have launched in Florida, from the Kennedy Space Center (KSC) on Merritt Island. Shuttles have rendezvoused with our Russian counterparts at least nine times and visited the International Space Station (ISS) over thirty-seven times throughout the duration.

ISS is a joint operation between the US, Russia, Japan, Europe, and Canada. The station is cut in half, with Russia operating one section and the other led by the US and shared by multiple nations. There has been someone there for the last twenty years.

On the private market, you have SpaceX launching a Falcon9 rocket which recently carried sixty satellites, and now has requested permission to launch at least 30,000 satellites and up to 42,000. Ponder that. Welcome to the new world of technology. The 'stated' goal is to provide internet service to those that are not connected.

The next launch just happened to be two days after I met Freddy, from Cape Canaveral Air Force Station. Cape Canaveral is across the street and a stone's throw (as they say) from Merritt Island. The public has been confused about Merritt Island, Kennedy Space Center, Cape Canaveral, and Cape Kennedy ever since Lyndon B

Johnson tried to get creative and changed their names after JFK's death. There are three launch pads between the areas—that's main thing to know.

Space shuttles/rockets launch from Florida due to its proximity to the equator, which allows them to send heavier equipment or go faster due to the earth's rotational spin.

I met with Tia and Aldo at a spacious VRBO beachfront home with line of sight access to Cape Canaveral. They arrived there the night before and Aldo elected to stay. I guess my intuition was correct.

I had requested aid from the President in getting clearance for the launch, with the one stipulation being that he could not ask why. He balked at first, but I reminded him that I technically didn't have to ask, and could have proceeded successfully on my own.

I was provided a private tour by Lt. Colonel Babs Goldfein despite that it had no open visitation to the public and was allowed to view up close the next rocket set to launch in the morning. My visit lasted another two hours as I was toured the base and other launch sites while observing where they built upcoming launches.

The three of us sipped on mimosas the next morning as we watched the successful launch of the Falcon 9, which is capable of reflight.

"Matti, I defer to you, but do you think that placing the vials there is the best option? So many unknowns...there could be equipment error, meteor strikes, or any kind of malfunction. Not to mention, the President himself aided you and now knows," Aldo asked intuitively.

"Yes, any of those could be a possibility. All these years, they have been unsuccessful at recreating their original creation. Maybe it's not meant for this world. Time will tell. In terms of the

President, let him think what he wants to think."

"Do you think those vials could provide other alternatives that were not considered?"

"I believe they do. You don't have this many agencies, countries, and deaths involved if there aren't more 'compelling' options."

Tia and I have known each other a long time. She came to train me when I was young and has stayed with my family ever since. She looks like a cross between Viola Davis and Octavia Spencer. She's brilliant, and is a master chess player. She had been observing me the whole time since we arrived. When Aldo excused himself to shower, she asked me to go to the balcony overseeing the ocean and put her arm through mine as we sat listening to the waves.

Three minutes passed before anything was said as we basked it the sunlight and fresh air. Finally, she turned to me and said, "Don't worry. I won't ever tell Aldo that you didn't place it there."

I feigned being shocked. "Why would you think that?"

"Child, I raised you. You wouldn't let Aldo or me be privy to this information…after everything that has happened, you wouldn't for our own safety, but I understand you needed to follow through for the perception to others."

I just winked and said, "I learned from the master herself."

What can I say? I have issues.

She left me to go to the kitchen and I started humming Eminem, *Fast Lane "…I don't really know where I'm headed, just enjoyin' the ride. Just gon' roll 'til I drop and ride 'til I die…"*

TWENTY-NINE

Pit Stop

WHILE I WAS IN FLORIDA, Bethany had some maintenance performed on our new 'lease' and also picked up some additional provisions we would be needing.

This was the first time that we were alone since it had all happened. Bethany and I had been together since training. There wasn't a day I didn't talk to her; she was an integral part of my life. I wondered how Freddy identified her to be my training roommate. Were there other hidden agendas with her selection? How much do I divulge? I resented Freddy for putting me in this situation, but ultimately, he didn't start this war.

I could have left the vials in Jerusalem forever. Maybe I should have. I could choose to destroy them and everything bad...or even good...that could result from their existence; or keep and hold them and hope that technology would catch up. I needed to consider wisely, and after the conversations with Freddy, I felt I was a little emotional and too connected to make a proper decision. A few more days or weeks was nothing compared to how long others had been searching.

We were on auto pilot on our way to CIA headquarters, flying into a private airfield in Washington, D.C. We were rehashing recent events and filling in the blanks.

To break the moment, I asked, "If you had to pick only one, what's your favorite all-time go-to movie?"

"Ahh, man, that's a hard one. So many to choose from, and it depends on the mood of the day. I'd say *Shawshank* rates up there at the top."

"I'd have to agree with you on that. I enjoyed *Inception,* too, but another one I love and watch every time it's on is *The American President.*"

"Good ones. I like your choices. Definitely a contrast to what your husband's favorite movie is," she said as we both laughed and simultaneously said, "*Notting Hill.*"

"There's nothing wrong with that one," I smiled.

"What's Steve's favorite movie?" I continued to inquire.

"I was wondering how long before you probed, nosy wench." She sneered. "Should have known something was up with the random question."

"It appears to be getting more serious. Well, just as in *The American President*, you better hope this goes all the way, or it could be damaging on many levels, not just for you."

"Don't think we haven't already discussed that. Trust me, we both understand."

"If you're having those conversations, I guess it must be getting serious. You know who I feel sorry for? His other girlfriend," I added.

"His other girlfriend? What the hell are you talking about!"

"Jake, of course, who did you think I meant?" I smiled again.

"Ha. Don't think that hasn't run across our conversations, too, but yeah, this time it feels different. Maybe it's because we are older, or it's just the right timing, being on a secluded beach for weeks. Breaks my heart to think Jake will be the only one without someone after all this time."

"We'll have to work on that."

"Listen, I know you think you are some super bad ass right now, all genetically modified and shit, but last time I checked, neither you nor I have any other real friends except each other, so how are you going to pull that off? And Mary is too young for him. Just saying."

"Leave my kid out of it, be'ach. We've been entrusted to save the world and protect our nation. Surely, we can find someone for him."

"True. If nothing else, we'll set up an account and just swipe left or right for him." She howled.

"You need help."

"You're my best friend, so what does that say?"

We both just laughed.

***

I had a meeting scheduled with Bill Sedlin, the Director of the CIA, and Mike Long, Deputy Director for Operations. They were assisting in providing me information that I had requested and, more importantly, that the President had ordered provided to me.

Truthfully, after the recent change in personnel at the CIA (mainly due to my efforts), I was glad I was able to have an open dialogue within the agency versus having to hack into their system or perform some other covert trick to obtain the information.

I did have to don a disguise to meet them, as the two of them recently attended my funeral. I opted for a classic look with a straight, blonde bob, a Halston crushed satin trench coat dress, and Tory Burch ankle boots, and met them at an Italian restaurant near headquarters, Café Oggi.

Sedlin and Long ordered a Glenfiddich neat, while I opted for a glass of Caymus Cabernet 2011. They asked if I wanted anything to eat, which I declined, saying I wouldn't be staying long.

Long passed a brown envelop across the table to me with 'confidential' stamped on top, while looking to Sedlin for affirmation.

I never understand why an intelligence agency that is delivering top-secret information would stamp, in big, bold, red lettering, 'CONFIDENTIAL' all over the file. Morons. I placed it in my handbag.

"Ms. Baker, you realize the severity of the information we are providing you—not just the agency, but for both of us personally," injected Sedlin.

I looked at him superciliously before calmly responding, "As I'm the inherent part of this, I think I should be privy to the details, and certainly have warranted and earned the rights. Don't you agree?"

"Of course. I didn't mean to infer you didn't," he responded, changing subjects quickly as he added, "When the time is right, if you'd like, we are able to assist in your resurrection, so to speak." I liked him. He seemed like a genuine guy and, more importantly, knew when to shut up.

"Thank you for your generous offer. I may take you up on that, but don't expect it to be any time soon. I need this time incognito."

"Ms. Baker, if you don't mind sharing, how did you know that we were not involved in any of this?" inquired Long.

"If you had knowledge of the project, you wouldn't have assisted me when I contacted you, but would've killed me instead."

We all took a sip of our drinks to reflect on that last statement. With that, I stood up, grabbed my purse, and shook their hands.

"Gentlemen, thank you for the drink. I'll be in touch."

I walked out to hail an Uber and eagerly awaited viewing the information that they provided me. I met Bethany at our favorite restaurant, Filomena, just twenty minutes down the road in Georgetown. Grandma can be seen in the window making homemade pasta, and their arancini balls are to die for. We ordered a Gaja Barbaresco while we scoured the menu that we knew by heart.

"Are you going to finally open it now, or are you just holding onto it for a keepsake?" Bethany asked.

"I already read it during the drive over here. This restaurant has a bevy of who's who, and couldn't take the risk."

"Spill it, woman."

"My two brothers operate under the identity of Jason and John, although that wasn't their original names. Jason was named David, and John was Jardani. It was a joint project between seven countries, with blind results to ensure that no one country could claim ownership. With my mother's last action, Jason went to the hands of the CIA, while Russia took John. They have been educated and trained with the best of the best under clandestine operations. Jason and John recently have gone rouge. Jason is believed to be in Europe, with John hiding out in Italy. They left a ton of wreckage in their wake before going MIA."

"Italy and Europe, huh? Will you have your new friends track them down?"

"I've asked a lot of them, recently. I'm not sure I want to be beholden to that right now. Since we now have more information on them, once we set up base, we'll want to explore first before enlisting any additional outside help. Plus, we need to keep our options open, just in case."

"Why do you think they went rogue now, after all this time? Do you think Aldo and the others already have knowledge or any affiliation?"

"Good questions. It's anyone's guess, right now. I'm looking forward to the day when I can discuss it with any of them."

"You doing ok? I mean, we haven't had a chance to talk about it, but you've been in a heap of shit lately, between Freddy not being your biological dad, your mom risking her and everyone else's lives on some secret project, you having two brothers, you're carrying a special DNA sequencing code, you organized to take out a squadron of perpetrators, you faked your own death…geez, I'm sure I'm leaving something out."

"Well, that would be a small squadron, by all accounts. Don't forget, I electively burned down my favorite dream house." I teased, trying to lighten the conversation.

"Well, your best friend is Anna Scott," she added, laughing.

"Really? *Notting Hill,* right now? Can't I get something more recent? *Terminator: Dark Fate* maybe? *Doctor Sleep,* even?"

"Nah, I'm sticking with that."

"I'm starting to question Steve's influence on you. Just saying."

"Lol. I know how you don't like to show emotion. You can process it all on your own time. Ok, let's change subjects. Where we headed now?"

"Let's think where we want to live, for the time being. I discussed it with Tom, and he wants Colorado. I was thinking North Carolina. What do you think?"

"Colorado? It's cold there eight months out of the year. We just left Montana and those frigid temperatures. Well, I did—you know, when I took care of your family. For a year. You remember that, right?" she added teasingly.

"Good god, woman, give it a rest. I should have left you there."

"Have you asked Freddy what he thinks?" She now turned serious in her inquiry.

"No, I haven't. Not yet. Once we get back into operation, I think we need to make some adjustments."

"I'm not sure I want to hear about that right now. How about we just enjoy this bottle." And she motioned to the wait staff to come over to order another. "My vote, not that you care, is to stay put with the white sandy beaches and warm weather."

"Now, B, that hurts my feelings. Of course I care, and your choice will be duly noted. Just make sure Steve wraps it up. I am not ready to be called Auntie."

"That would be the second coming of Christ if it happened, so you would call me 'Oh glorious one almighty' if it does."

"Please Stop. I have not had enough to drink."

THIRTY

Hideaway

KNOWING HOW BETHANY HATED cold temperatures, she wasn't thrilled when I said we needed to make an alternate stop first before heading back to the family. She had made the necessary requirements for the plane to accommodate the colder weather we were venturing into, but she was still not a fan of the notion that we had to fly to Greenland to refuel before heading to Longyear Airport in Norway, of all places.

I had been carrying the vials with me twenty-four/seven since their return. I knew this wasn't the most practical or logical solution and also knew I'd have to ensure their longer-term safety elsewhere.

Our seven scientists visited Antarctica, and we still have not confirmed the intent of their visit. It did direct me to think of an opportunity to store the vials on the other side of the continent, in the Arctic Circle. In tundra weather, in a remote location visible only by an odd-shaped structure sticking out of the ground with a short walkway, lies the Svalbard Global Seed Vault, operated by the Norwegian government.

The seed vault is a long-term depository that has deposits from all across the globe. It now has over one million varietals for essential food crops and plant species. It was established in 2008 to help in event of mismanagement, natural disasters, equipment failure, etc., but it has been largely been speculated that its true intent was to help rebuild in the event of a large-scale or global catastrophe. It's like the hidden bunker portrayed in *Deep Impact*, but in Norway.

Norway's allies happen to include the US. They do not include Russia, China, or Afghanistan. The Norwegian government funds the upkeep with support from some hefty donors.

Each sample deposited consists of over five hundred seeds in airtight three-ply pouches, stored in tote containers, on metal shelving racks at temperatures from negative one degree Celsius. It was the perfect environment for my deposit. The facility has a current capacity to host over four million samples. They operate similar to a safe deposit box. Only you can access your deposit, and no one else's. I'd be depositing under the alias of Elizabeth Smith with some outside assistance from their significant donor, Bill and Melinda Gates.

Only Bethany and Tom knew of my visit here. I trusted Aldo implicitly, as we had twenty years collaborating. Bessum and Lily had proved their worth over the last weeks, but they were affiliated with the Albanian and Sicilian mob. Just saying. I would never be family at the end of the day, and couldn't afford any risks.

Often, in military or business, it is cost effective to create two of something when only one is needed. What if the scientists had their own version of this idea on the other side of the continent? I'd need to return and explore further, when time permitted.

I couldn't help but think of the old-time classic song Secret Agent Man by Johnny Rivers, about the life of a spy... *"With every move he makes, another chance he takes. Odds are he won't live to see tomorrow..."*

I had beaten the odds, over and over. It was time to return to my new home.

THIRTY-ONE

Home Sweet Home

WITH OUR WHIRLWIND TRAVELS and errands out of the way, we headed back to the stunning views of Ihla. We spent another month enjoying all the scenery and beauty of the remote island. The surf was strong, and the kids became quite proficient at surfing. We all settled into a comfortable routine that we sadly knew was coming to an end. Days were spent exploring and snorkeling (I passed on the snorkeling, most days) and nights involved playing Mexican Train or Cards Against Humanity (my parents opted out of the latter).

My parents were the first to depart to return home to Montgomery, Mississippi. Dad was asked to consult in the athletic department and Mom had her church group and community service groups she was active in. Tia returned with them, but had already made plans to travel to Italy to visit Aldo. She had done so much for my family over the years, I was glad to see that she was doing something for herself. She deserved to be happy.

Jake and Steve were the next to leave. The boys needed to prepare for the upcoming training session that they would be starting. We had identified two other males and one female prospect that we thought would be a good fit with the kids (and, more importantly, the program). No longer based out of Minot, the new location was in Montgomery, Alabama near Maxwell AFB. It was also only a four-hour drive from Grandma and Grampy. We didn't want them trained like Bethany and I had experienced, like robots, but we wanted all to have a balanced life—well, as much as you can, being a trained counter-terrorism contract operative.

The following week, Bethany flew the kids out to their new accommodations with Jake and Steve. Tom and I had the same reservations and feelings we did when we dropped them off to training originally—probably more so, based on recent events. Part of us wanted them to stay with us forever. If only they wouldn't grow up. Who were we kidding? They already were. They are the next generation, and were eager and ready to take charge.

Tom and I purchased land outside of Dallas, Texas in a small town called Southlake. We finally agreed to this location because it was smack dab in the middle of the country with easy access to airports, but secluded enough, still, for privacy. With only thirty thousand people, it was a ten-minute commute to the DFW Airport or twenty minutes to a private air strip. We would use this house as a hub for the kids, while still allowing us to lock and leave to venture to new cities. We purchased twenty acres to build a main house with two additional guest houses.

I was envisioning a house like Diane Keaton had in *Something's Gotta Give,* or maybe Meryl Streep in *It's Complicated.* One of the guest houses was for Freddy, who would be moving in at the end of the month following his release from the hospital and physical therapy. It was time to get to know this man, who had devoted his entire life to the survival of mine. I also needed and wanted to learn more about my mother.

The best part of this new home was that it was in an exemplary school district, and even though we no longer had school-age kids, they had a dominating presence in football, cross country, swimming, and diving, with multiple State Championships. Nothing better than high school sports, in my humble opinion, and I couldn't wait to go cheer them on.

On the last evening before our departure from Ihla, Tom and I sat outside on the double recliner holding hands, gazing at the stars, and listening to a little music. Depeche Mode was playing, his favorite. He walked inside and came back with a bottle of Abacus. My eyes twinkled in excitement. We normally shared this bottle of wine before or after a mission. I felt something building.

"Interesting selection you have there, Mr. Baker," I said as I slid my hand back into his.

"I thought it was appropriate. Have you enjoyed our time here?" he asked earnestly.

"Of course, babe. No one I would rather be with."

"You're not bored?" he continued to probe.

"Well, I'm not sure I'd say bored, but I am getting a little fidgety."

"I thought as much. I made a call on the sat comm while you were saying good-bye to the kids. It seems your presence has been requested by The President. It appears they need your assistance on an urgent new matter."

This man. He knows me so well. He makes my heart melt. I just smiled at him in admiration and longing.

"If Momma isn't happy, no one is. Trust me, I know. Let's toast to new adventures," he said as he raised his glass.

The music changed and Tom Petty's *Running Down a Dream* was now playing... *"Yeah, running down a dream that never would come to me, working on a mystery, and doin' wherever it leads, runnin' down a dream..."*

We clinked glasses and I took a sip. "I love you, babe. You do realize we have no kids or other people here? I have an idea…" I said as I ran towards the water with him chasing me.

THE NEXT CHAPTER

I WAS IN THE STUDY with the Tracker TS45 gun safe open. This can hold up to 45 guns, but was nothing compared to the secret room that was being built in the new house. I was cleaning a Sig Sauer P226X5 when the secure line rang. I took my time and picked it up on the third ring.

"Going forward, you'll be reporting to me and me only. Is that acceptable?"

"My. President, I took an oath many years ago. Technically, I've always been working in some capacity for you," I responded.

The oath of enlistment is a federal law. Anyone who enlists in armed forces is required to take it. It states: {I (state your name) do solemnly swear (or affirm) that I will support and defend the constitution of the United States against all enemies, foreign and domestic; that I will bear true faith and allegiance to the same; and that I will obey the orders of the President of the United States and the orders of the officers appointed over me, according to the regulations and the uniform code of military justice. So help me God.}

"I'm on a time crunch on this, Ms. Baker. I'm counting on you to bring this to fruition quickly," the President added.

"I serve at the pleasure of the President."

"Godspeed, Matti. We're counting on you."

My computer pinged. As I looked at the confidential encrypted file that was just sent to me, I put on some music to set the tone. Eminem, Lose Yourself... *"This world is mine for the taking, Make me king, as we move toward a new world order..."*

The United Nations recognizes 241 countries in the world. The US recognizes 195. Come on, people, can't we agree on anything? Twenty-two countries use lobbyists to help push specific legislation, and the US is one of the biggest proponents, with much heated discussion on both sides of the political spectrum (9% or 11%, depending on which figure you stand behind).

We would be focusing on the biggest spenders, which typically were large corporations (GE, Proctor and Gamble, Honeywell, 3M...) that occur at every level; federal, state, county, municipality and even local governments.

The United States accounts for 12,000 lobbyists representing roughly 300 law firms, with pharmaceutical/health products outpacing all other industries. Due to the extensive rules and potential penalties to lobbyists, they were advancing their tactics and using sophisticated strategies to hide their activity. Other countries quickly cued into that. Go figure.

Any time you have a paid organization with the purpose of influencing a political office or outcome for a desired legislation, this equals MONEY, the root of all evil.

China has quickly become the world's biggest pharmacy, and I suspected our own FDA was involved in this coup, as well. Another damn 'A' agency or country.

So, let's look at our pals at the FDA. The FDA falls under the Department of Health and Human Services, one of fifteen branches under the executive branch. These heads of states are the arms of the President of the US.

The FDA regulates: Food, drugs, medical devices, vaccines, animals, cosmetics, and last but not least, the tobacco industry.

Previously, the only conversations being discussed and heard were about opioids, with over 70,000 deaths just last year. Where was the regulation and legislation when doctors/states were handing consumers opioids like they were tic-tacs? Purdue Pharma, founded by the Sackler Brothers, introduced oxycontin in the 1980s, when they heavily lobbied lawmakers for the treatment of chronic pain. As a result, consumers developed a tolerance to the drugs, which then led to addiction.

This year, the US has had thirty-nine vaping deaths, and all kinds of new legislation is being introduced and products are being taken off the market. Why?

Lobbyists. Big money corporations. It's simple smoke and mirrors.

When you mess with mother nature, you don't know what you will get. Trust me, I'm a living example of this. It's why the potential outcome and devastation of eugenics/CRISPR is scary. When you start taking vitamins, your body now relies on vitamins and stops producing its own. You lose the craving to eat what your body needs to absorb, be it vegetables, fruit, etc. If you start taking thyroid medicine, your body stops producing it naturally. Allergies are prominent, now. Why? Too many antibiotics killed our body's ability to fight infections on its own. Why do you think there are so many erectile dysfunction commercials, now? Just saying.

And, its big business regulated by the FDA. Close to three million people get sick from drug-resistant 'superbug' infections every year. Thirty-five thousand will die as a result. For legal reasons, it's cheaper to kill than to maim.

It can cost you five dollars a pill for an antibiotic, which is ten cents in other countries. Or, plan an additional forty-five dollars for Cialis in the U.S. when you can get it for fifteen cents in Amsterdam.

China accounts for seventy percent of the pharmaceutical market, with most US generic medicines manufactured over there.

The US's growing dependence on China opens a window for China to use this as a weapon against us. Looking at China from a national security perspective, the US has decided that the best approach is to ensure safety and effectiveness. The FDA has been charged to expand inspection and regulation.

Lobbyists have other objectives. F'in lobbyists. With new tariffs placed on China, we're playing Russian roulette.

The Commissioner of the FDA is Roman Wagner. Roman is a name dating back to the Roman empire, and biblically means 'powerful.' His best friend is Chanlor Wilson, who happens to be the top lobbyist for the medical industry…

Whitesnake is playing in my head… *Here I Go Again…"Tho' I keep searching for an answer, I never seem to find what I'm looking for…"*

NOTE FROM THE AUTHOR

Every magic trick has three parts. You may have remembered this from *The Prestige* with Christian Bale and Hugh Jackman. (Of course, the movie *The Illusionists*, with Edward Norton and Jessica Biel, was great, too.)

In the first part, called the pledge, the magicians shows you something ordinary. During the second part, the turn, they take the ordinary and make it extraordinary. The hardest part is the third act, the prestige. Why? Because you want to be fooled.

I hope you enjoyed the storytelling in the Matti Baker series: AESOP, FABLE, and TELLER.

It's been fun playing off daily news, events, and real conspiracies, intertwining these details with my personal life. The best part is, it doesn't have to end. Did you like how I tied in Jason Bourne and John Wick? How clever was that? Can you say new FRANCHISE?!

If you've enjoyed these books and want to read more about Matti Baker, take a moment to leave a review on any of the book sites (like Amazon or Goodreads), or share with a friend, or share with any of your famous book or movie publishing friends. (Sharing is caring.)

Or, visit www.michelepackard.com and leave a note saying #morematti

Until then,

– MP

I'd like to thank the following movies and songs which inspired the tone and backdrop throughout this series. (P.S. Don't be a jerk and try to sue for copyright infringement. A simple "Thank You" would be nice)

Per copy right regulations: You can use extracts of a copyright work for purposes of parody, caricature or pastiche, provided that:

- *the use is fair dealing;*
- *you rely on no more than a limited, moderate amount of the underlying work;*
- *you include proper acknowledgement (generally the title and the author's name).*

Movies and Shows

The Crying Game 12 Strong
60 Minutes
Ad Astra
Angels and Demons
Armageddon
Bone Collector
Braveheart
Captain America
Castaway
Cocktail
Conspiracy Theory
Days of Thunder
Deep Impact
Designated Survivor
Dirty Dancing
Enemy at the Gates
Enemy of the State
Equalizer
Fifty Shades
For the Love of the Game
Forget Paris
Friday the 13th
Full Metal Jacket
Games of Thrones
Godfather
Gone in 60 Seconds

Great Gatsby
Home Alone
House of Cards
Hunger Games
Hunt for Red October
Inception
Independence Day
Indiana Jones and Last Crusade
It's Complicated
Jarhead
Jungle Fever
Jurassic Park
Justice League Wonder Women
Knight and Day
Love Actually
Man in the High Castle
Men in Black
Mission Impossible franchise
Money Heist
Mr. and Mrs. Smith
Notting Hill
Omen
Pelican Brief
Quantum of Solace
Rambo
Roadhouse

Saving Private Ryan
Scarface
Sins of My Father
Sixth Sense
Sniper
Somethings Gott Give
Speed
Taken
The Blind Side

The Hitman
The Hunt for Red October
The Sound of Music
The Sum of All Fears

Shawshank Redemption
Shooter
The Untouchables
The Wizard of Oz
Top Gun
Trading Places
U-571
Vanilla Sky
Veep
Wallstreet
Wedding Crashers
Weekend at Bernies
West Wing

Songs

Awesome God
Blow up the Outside World
Boys are Back in Town
Bring me to Life
Creep
Criminal
Fast Lane
Feeling Good
Gangster of Paradise
Here I go Again
Hot Potato
I Ran
I'm Waking Up
It's My Life
Look What you made me do
Lose Yourself
Love the Way you Lie
Machinehead
Nessum Dorma
Psycho

Running Down a Dream
Secret Agent
Shameless
Somebody
Song of Someone
Stronger
Take it Easy
Take Me Home Tonight
Thanksgiving
The End
The Final Countdown
Time in a Bottle
Timewarp
U & Ur Hand
Welcome to the Jungle
When I said I Do
When the Sun Goes Down
You are the Love of my Life
You Got Another Thing Coming
You Oughta Know

ABOUT THE AUTHOR

Michele Packard comes from a military family and worked tirelessly as a cable tv executive before staying at home to raise her three children. She has written in both the fiction and non-fiction genres, utilizing her experiences and wit to share stories with others. Her debut novel, AESOP, won 1st place from Pencraft in the Fiction/Thriller/Terrorist category and was a finalist in American Book Festival and Independent Author Network Awards. She is a frequent traveler with her husband and is the primary caretaker of the family's beloved labs.

Join Michele's newsletter and receive updates, discounts, new book launches, and receive a free copy of her book SNIDBITS (a completely inappropriate book).

Follow for more information and insights:
www.michelepackard.com
Instagram: @aesopstories
Goodreads: @michelepackard

Yo, Adrian, we did it!

I'll be right back.

Made in the USA
Middletown, DE
11 April 2022

64020972R10102